In the Making

G. F. Green was born in Derbyshire in 1911. His short stories of working-class life in the industrial north of England appeared in numerous periodicals and anthologies during the 1930s and were published in volume form as *Land Without Heroes* (1948). During the war he served in what was then Ceylon, in the commander-in-chief's public-relations department, where he edited *Veera Lanka*, a magazine for the Ceylonese forces. In 1944 he was court-martialled, cashiered and sentenced to two years' imprisonment for homosexual offences. He suffered a breakdown after his release from Wakefield Prison, but recovered after becoming a patient of the psychiatrist Dr Charlotte Wolff, who encouraged him to start writing again. He edited an anthology of stories on the theme of childhood, *First View* (1950), and completed a novel, *In the Making* (1952). In 1957 he settled in Somerset and, after a long silence, published a triptych of novellas, *The Power of Sergeant Streater* (1972). The stories he was writing for a further volume when he died in 1977 were collected, along with extracts from his other books and the reminiscences of friends, in *A Skilled Hand* (1980).

Peter Parker was born in Herefordshire and, like G. F. Green, went to prep school in the Malvern Hills. He is the author of two books on the First World War, *The Old Lie* (1987) and *The Last Veteran* (2009), and biographies of J. R. Ackerley (1989) and Christopher Isherwood (2004). He edited *A Reader's Guide to the Twentieth-Century Novel* (1995) and *A Reader's Guide to Twentieth-Century Writers* (1996). He was an associate editor of the *Oxford Dictionary of National Biography* (2004), with responsibility for modern literature, and remains an advisory editor. Since 1979 he has been a regular contributor of book reviews and features to numerous newspapers and magazines, including *The Sunday Times*, the *Daily Telegraph*, *The TLS* and *HORTUS*. An animated film of J. R. Ackerley's book *My Dog Tulip*, for which he collaborated on the script and acted as adviser to the producers, was released in 2010.

G. F. GREEN

In the Making

The Story of a Childhood

Introduction by PETER PARKER

PENGUIN BOOKS

PENGUIN CLASSICS

Published by the Penguin Group
Penguin Books Ltd, 80 Strand, London WC2R ORL, England
Penguin Group (USA) Inc., 375 Hudson Street, New York, New York 10014, USA
Penguin Group (Canada), 90 Eglinton Avenue East, Suite 700, Toronto, Ontario, Canada M4P 2Y3
(a division of Pearson Penguin Canada Inc.)
Penguin Ireland, 25 St Stephen's Green, Dublin 2, Ireland (a division of Penguin Books Ltd)
Penguin Group (Australia), 250 Camberwell Road, Camberwell, Victoria 3124, Australia
(a division of Pearson Australia Group Pty Ltd)
Penguin Books India Pvt Ltd, 11 Community Centre, Panchsheel Park, New Delhi – 110 017, India
Penguin Group (NZ), 67 Apollo Drive, Rosedale, Auckland 0632, New Zealand
(a division of Pearson New Zealand Ltd)
Penguin Books (South Africa) (Pty) Ltd, 24 Sturdee Avenue, Rosebank,
Johannesburg 2196, South Africa

Penguin Books Ltd, Registered Offices: 80 Strand, London WC2R ORL, England

www.penguin.com

First published in Great Britain by Peter Davies Ltd 1952
This edition published in Penguin Classics 2012
1

Copyright 1952 by G. F. Green
Introduction copyright © Peter Parker, 2012
All rights reserved

The moral right of the author and the author of the introduction has been asserted

Set in Dante MT Std 10.5/13 pt
Typeset by Palimpsest Book Production Limited, Falkirk, Stirlingshire
Printed in Great Britain by Clays Ltd, St Ives plc

ISBN: 978-0-141-19757-9

www.greenpenguin.co.uk

Penguin Books is committed to a sustainable
future for our business, our readers and our
planet. This book is made from paper certified
by the Forest Stewardship Council.

Contents

Introduction

In the Making is subtitled 'The Story of a Childhood' and describes the experiences undergone between the ages of five and fourteen by a boy called Randal Thane. Much of the novel takes place at Randal's preparatory school, where he falls unwillingly but hopelessly under the spell of a slightly older boy called Felton. The result is one of the most sophisticated, unusual and devastating school stories you are ever likely to read. While 'romantic friendships' have been a regular feature of novels set in boarding schools, they do not often take place between boys as young as those in Green's story. More usually such novels are set in public schools and reflect what Alec Waugh (whose *The Loom of Youth* caused a huge scandal in 1917) referred to as 'the inevitable emotional consequences of a monastic herding together for eight months of the year of thirteen-year-old children and eighteen-year-old adolescents'.[1] By Waugh's standard, both Randal and Felton are children, and the inequality between them is not one of age but one of apprehension.

Green was well aware that the book was sailing 'too near every wind', but he was annoyed when critics concentrated on its subject matter rather than the highly wrought prose in which it is written.[2] 'It seems that a great many people simply don't regard the *writing*,' he complained: 'a book might as well be a précis of a story – or a strip cartoon. When you consider that Flaubert said "The style is all" – it makes me wonder. Personally I'm *quite* convinced that the style *is* all.'[3] It is the sheer quality of the writing that sets *In the Making* apart from most school stories. In conception and execution it has more in common with the work of Elizabeth Bowen and Henry James, two writers who also wrote superbly about children, than it has with such celebrated school romances as H. A. Vachell's *The Hill* (1905) or E. F. Benson's *David Blaize* (1916).

'No one who cares for writing and equally no one who cares for life should miss *Land Without Heroes*,' Bowen declared, when Green's first book, a collection of short stories, appeared in 1948, and the same might be said of *In the Making*.[4] It was with stories about working-class life in the industrial north of England that Green began his career as a published writer. They appeared in all the right places in the 1930s: the *London Mercury*, the *Spectator*, the *Listener*, *New Writing*, *New Stories*, *Penguin New Writing*, *Horizon*. Although some of them dealt with arson, horrific industrial accidents, and even murder among children, few of them were straightforward narratives. Almost everything was in the writing, and Green rightly saw nothing inappropriate about using compression, elision and exhilarating syntactical complexity to represent the outwardly ordinary lives of foundrymen and their families. His near namesake, Henry Green, was doing something similar in such novels as *Living* (1929), but G. F. Green felt that his own method was 'extremely visual, using gesture and physical detail to convey the meaning' and owed 'more to the cinema than to other writers'.[5] His reputation during this period stood high: Bowen solicited work from him when editing *The Faber Book of Modern Stories* in 1937, Cyril Connolly included him in his *Horizon Stories* in 1943, and his work appeared in Jonathan Cape's annual *Best Short Stories* anthologies in 1936, 1938, 1939 and 1940. By the time these stories were collected in a single volume, followed in 1952 by *In the Making*, Green had attracted a formidable array of admirers: E. M. Forster, Christopher Isherwood, Stephen Spender, J. R. Ackerley, John Lehmann, John Betjeman, Philip Toynbee, C. P. Snow, Pamela Hansford Johnson, Frank Tuohy and Alan Sillitoe. Bowen once described him as 'the most neglected writer of his generation'.[6] He still is. Some thirty years after his death, not one of his books was in print – until now.

This is not a case of a once popular or fashionable writer disappearing from view because literary tastes have changed. Green was always, in that double-edged phrase, a writers' writer, greatly admired by fellow-practitioners but never achieving much in the way of sales or wider fame. He always found writing a struggle and published comparatively little during his lifetime. 'Each story is perfect in its own right,' Philip Toynbee wrote, when reviewing *Land Without Heroes* in the *New Statesman*, 'cleverly planned, beautifully executed and leaving, one guesses, the precise impression which Mr Green intended.'[7] Leaving the precise impression was a long and hard process, involving almost constant revision through many drafts, sometimes over many years. Even then, a number of novels and stories were completed and then discarded because they did not meet his exacting standards. Green often accused himself (unfairly) of laziness, and (more justly) recognized that the amount he drank at certain periods of his life interfered with his writing. His working life was also interrupted by rootlessness (he had no permanent home of his own until he was in his late forties), war service, imprisonment and a mental breakdown.

George Frederick Green (always known to family and friends as Dick) was born in Derbyshire in 1911. The son of a prosperous iron-founder, he was sent to the Wells House preparatory school in the Malvern Hills, continuing his education at Repton and Magdalene College, Cambridge, where he read English. It was at Cambridge that he met the future actor Michael Redgrave, with whom he would always remain very close. The two men saw each other as often as Redgrave's busy professional and personal life permitted, and corresponded regularly when apart. Green dedicated his first book to Redgrave, acted as best man at his wedding, and became godfather of his first child, Vanessa. He had already embarked on the novel that would later become *In the Making* while still an undergraduate, and would show Redgrave almost all his work in progress. Partly cushioned by family money, he was never in full-time employment, although in order to make ends meet he took a number of short-lived part-time jobs: private tutoring, occasional reviewing, ghost-writing the autobiography of an Italian marchesa. He pursued a bohemian existence in London, but returned often to Derbyshire, making forays into the village of Old Whittington, where he carefully observed, listened to and conversed with local people, gathering material for the short stories he published in the 1930s.

Called up in 1940, he joined the ranks of the 3rd Suffolk Infantry Regiment and characteristically fell in love with his platoon's lance-corporal while in training in Warwickshire. After further training with the Officer Cadet Training Unit in North Wales, he became a second lieutenant and was posted to what was then Ceylon, where he served as aide-de-camp to the brigadier before being transferred to the commander-in-chief's public-relations department. He became editor of a magazine for the Ceylonese forces called *Veera Lanka*, published in both Tamil and Sinhalese. This job was not onerous, largely consisting of getting material from Britain and having it translated. Much of his time was spent travelling round what he called 'this paradise of an island', whose people he grew to love – ostensibly to gather stories for the magazine.[8] Back at headquarters in Colombo, he devoted his spare time to 'verandahism', an all-embracing term he coined for drinking, smoking, taking Benzedrine and conducting liaisons with local youths on a verandah he had commandeered and converted for his private use. His intake of drink and drugs made him careless and he was eventually caught *in flagrante* with a Sinhalese rickshaw-puller. He was court-martialled, cashiered and sentenced to two years' imprisonment. He served the first months in an old colonial jail on the island, during which time he kept a diary. This became the basis of an article entitled 'Military Detention', which would be published in *Penguin New Writing* in 1947 under the pseudonym 'Lieut. Z'. In February 1945 Green was transferred to Wakefield Prison in Yorkshire, where he served the remainder of his sentence.

Released in 1946, he suffered a breakdown and, although supported by friends such as Redgrave and by his elder brother John and sister-in-law Chloë, to whom he was particularly close, he was hardly able to function at all. It was on Redgrave's recommendation that he became a patient of the well-known psychiatrist Charlotte Wolff, who helped him recover both his sense of identity and his ability to write, in particular encouraging him to take out and revise his long-abandoned prep-school novel. *In the Making* was published four years after the appearance of *Land Without Heroes*, and between these two volumes Green edited a fine anthology of short stories about childhood, *First View* (1950), which he dedicated to the memory of Denton Welch, a writer he greatly admired. He nevertheless remained restless during this period, wandering from place to place, relying often upon the hospitality of friends and family, and still indulging in bouts of heavy and destructive drinking. In 1957 a legacy from an uncle allowed him to settle in the Somerset village of Batcombe, where he bought and restored a house and created a formal Italianate garden. He worked slowly here on *The Power of Sergeant Streater* (1972), a triptych of inter-related novellas set in Derbyshire and south-east Asia, and a volume of short stories on the theme of betrayal in love, set in Ceylon and Morocco. Diagnosed with terminal lung cancer, he chose to take his own life in his own time and died in 1977. The five stories he completed before his death were published alongside extracts from his other books, interspersed with 'memoirs and criticism' by those who knew and admired him, in a volume titled *A Skilled Hand* (1980), edited by Chloë Green and the publisher A. D. Maclean.

Everything Green wrote can be warmly recommended, but *In the Making* is his masterpiece. The subject was one that required delicate handling, but Green was determined not to fudge the issue. Randal may not fully comprehend the nature of his intense need to 'possess' Felton, but Green certainly did. 'To write of homosexual love as if it were – which in fact it is – normal, is to thread a way through a laby-rinth of disasters', he told Chloë Green while extensively revising the novel. 'It needs a very pure mind – in the sense of exact, just, full of integrity. For the least failure in such a theme is to tumble the whole edifice down. It *has* to be right.'[9] These are the words of a craftsman rather than those of a moralist, and throughout his career Green remained obsessed by finding the right language in which his subject matter could reveal itself. 'The transferring of a theme into writing sometimes seems to me almost impossibly difficult,' he complained. 'How is one to choose this word and that way – out of countless possibilities?'[10] It was these dilemmas that caused Green to take so long to finish *In the Making* to his satisfaction.

He had put aside the version of the novel he completed in the early 1930s after it was turned down by several publishers, and without the encouragement of Charlotte Wolff it might have remained in the bottom drawer. 'Impossible to say what Charlotte has done,' he told Redgrave. 'It's as if she's awoken one out of a drugged sleep & here one finds everything *fresh* new yet familiar and vastly interesting – and full of possibilities.'[11] In order to realize those possibilities, Green would take somewhat longer to revise the book than the fortnight Wolff had suggested was needed. Four months later he was still involved in a 'hell of a lot of re-writing' and was 'doing an entirely new section of 12,000 words'.[12] This new section would become Part Three of the novel, in which the two boys attend the school's Hallowe'en fancy-dress party. Although this scene was a late addition to the novel, Green immediately recognized its importance: 'I can't think how I came not to write such a wonderful *and apt* scene in the first place,' he told Redgrave.[13] It would provide the 'perfect climax' to the relationship between the two boys: 'If I can feel sure that this is right, then the rest of the book can follow its own course'.[14] Getting it right took time, however. The section grew to 20,000 words, and had to be rewritten twice: 'After the first revision I came to re-read & found that I had systematically removed all the magic – all the original "flair" – and had left a kind of précis', he told Chloë. 'I was absolutely floored. The only thing to do was to start all over again and put back most of what I'd taken out. This I've done. I'm sure the original *needed* revision, but whether I've done too much & in any way killed the *dream* effect I just don't know.'[15]

It would be the culmination of a succession of richly imagined and indeed dream-like set pieces in which Green charts the relationship between Randal and Felton. Randal's almost hyperaesthetic perception of his surroundings is a manifestation of his passionate feelings for Felton, wonderfully evoking the transformative power of love. The two boys go tobogganing in a deserted combe on a snow-muffled half-holiday; they take trips through the countryside on summer evenings with a doting master in his car; and they appear as Pierrot and Harlequin at the spectacular Hallowe'en party. In each of these scenes, even at the crowded party, Green conveys the sense of time being suspended, the Metaphysical notion of two lovers creating and inhabiting a private world.

When Green told Michael Redgrave that he had decided on *In the*

Making as a title, adding that 'the theme is unequivocally that of the conditioning of a homosexual & the foreshadowing of his future love pattern', he was still being treated by Charlotte Wolff and evidently using the language of her profession.[16] The word 'pattern' does, however, recur throughout the novel, building to its final sentence. Pattern additionally provides Green with a way of telling his story, just as he used what he thought of as cinematic techniques in his earlier short stories. While its narrative is traditionally linear, the novel makes elaborate use of verbal echoes and reflecting images that bind it into an intricately faceted whole. The very opening of the novel, in which five-year-old Randal kneels before the nursery fire, immediately plunges us into the boy's secret world and plants images and words in the reader's mind that will resonate throughout the book: not just the fire, tassels, cords and fingers – all of which recur and are highlighted at crucial moments later in the book – but 'indifferent', 'possess' and 'enslave'. Few novels – apart, perhaps, from Henry Green's *Caught* (1943), which is set in the Blitz – contain as many carefully deployed images of light and fire. They are particularly associated with Felton, and Randal will come to understand that light can both illuminate and dazzle, while fire both warms and scorches. In the nursery Randal is able to expose himself to the fire, a 'tiger' safely caged behind the fender, and feel the comfort of its heat 'pressed against his body' without getting burned. This sense of precarious security resurfaces throughout the book, notably when the boys go tobogganing and Randal, 'held by Felton entirely, alone with him', lies in the snow, pressing his face into his friend's thick sweater.

While steering carefully away from anything explicitly sexual in the boys' relationship, Green nevertheless needed to convey the erotic quality of Randal's feelings. Clothes, and more particularly the contrasting feel of clothes and bare skin, are therefore lovingly dwelt upon throughout the novel, from the boys' hugely glamorous school uniform – consisting of a white shirt and pullover, white shorts held up by a red snake-clasp belt, and a red blazer – to Randal's rippling silk Pierrot costume and the 'skin-tight diamonds' and hair-snagging domino of Felton's Harlequin outfit in the crucial and climactic Hallowe'en episode. An example of Green's masterful handling of material is the scene in which Randal, 'against all the evening's rules', seizes an apple that has been suspended on a string in preparation for a party-game, in order to share it with Felton. While this clearly carries symbolic weight, it is at the same time entirely appropriate to the setting – and both the elaborate fancy-dress party and the beautiful red-and-white school uniform were features of the Wells House at the time. From the moment Randal opens the door into the hall where the party is taking place to 'an arc of gold shouts and lights and heat which swung in his face like a fist of gilded mail', the Hallowe'en episode is a descriptive *tour de force* in which Green uses language to near-hallucinatory effect. The reader is as dazzled and beguiled as Randal is, drawn into a heightened world that the boy has created.

Charlotte Wolff was perhaps nearer the mark when she called the novel 'an enchantment', for it both describes and embodies that word, rather as *A Midsummer Night's Dream* does.[17] The spell is eventually broken, and while Randal 'never discovered that this happiness, keener perhaps than any he would experience again, was derived from his own imagination', this does not, for Green, devalue that happiness or the imagination that created it. The experience would, he suggests in the novel's closing words, be the making of Randal as a person and a writer – as it was for Green himself.

One of the reasons Green never strikes a false note in the novel is that he never patronizes his young characters, basing Randal's experiences closely on his own. One of his school-fellows, John Marshall, noted that 'the school scenes, places, and characters all existed in life'.[18] Green may have relocated his fictional school to Somerset, but it is telling that he forgot to alter references to 'the Roman Camp' and a cottage 'where Jenny Lind had once lived', both of which are features of the Malvern Hills rather than the Quantocks. The co-ordinates of Randal's heart, however, almost exactly matched those of Green. Marshall added that the model for Felton was 'a well-knit athletic boy with no spiritual interests. He was generally considered to be "topping" because of his athleticism and bravura. It was the bravura that got Dick, and Randal's emotions were certainly real. Dick himself had very few dealings with Felton – his anguish only bore fruit in an unusual school-story thirty years later. A happy ending, really.'[19]

Notes

1. Alec Waugh, *The Loom of Youth* (London: Geoffrey Bles, rev. edn., 1955), p. 12.

2. Unpublished letter to Chloë Green, 25 May 1948.

3. *ibid.*, 30 October 1952.

4. *Tatler*, 4 February 1948.

5. See dustjacket of *Land Without Heroes* by G. F. Green (London: Home & Van Thal, 1948).

6. Quoted in anonymous obituary of G. F. Green, *The Times* (London), 15 August 1977.

7. Philip Toynbee, review for *Land Without Heroes*, *New Statesman and Nation* magazine, 28 February 1948.

8. Unpublished letter to Michael Redgrave, 8 September 1942.

9. Unpublished letter to Chloë Green, 25 May 1948.

10. *ibid.*

11. Unpublished letter to Michael Redgrave, 14 December 1946.

12. *ibid.*, 26 April 1947.

13. *ibid.*, 14 December 1946.

14. Unpublished letter to Chloë Green, 25 May 1948.

15. *ibid.*

16. Unpublished letter to Michael Redgrave, 14 December 1946.

17. Quoted in unpublished letter to Michael Redgrave, 14 December 1946.

18. John Marshall, in *A Skilled Hand*, ed. Chloë Green and A. D. Maclean (London: Macmillan, 1980), p. 17.

19. *ibid.*

Acknowledgements

Peter Parker would like to thank Richard Canning, Edward Behrens, Niall Hobhouse and, above all, Chloë Green. Thanks are also due to the Board of Trustees of the Victoria and Albert Museum, Theatre and Performance Collections, for permission to consult the Sir Michael Redgrave Archive (THM/31); and to Chelsea Weathers at the Harry Ransom Humanities Research Center, the University of Texas at Austin.

In the Making

To My Mother and Father

Tu ne me chercherais pas si tu ne me possédais.
Ne t'inquiète donc pas.

Pascal

PART ONE

Peradventure

In Randal's nursery the fire roared and leapt at the black tunnel of chimney, whilst Randal, kneeling before the tall fender with his fingers between the trellises, was an Indian Prince watching his caged and fiery tiger. His dressing-gown was open so that the tiger's heat pressed against his body, but the loose cords and tassels of his royal cloak hung indifferent to the frenzied beast. The fire began to possess his stomach and legs and sting his face. He pressed his fingers tighter into the wires, pretending to be trapped in the cage, enslaved by the fiery demon who was ready to devour him. When the heat made him blink, he released himself and turning, lay back against the fender. 'Slain,' he whispered.

The shadows fell huge on the walls. Crouching beneath his dressing-gown, he stared at them plunging along the stretch of light, where the young adventurers went by in the frieze, travelling in full company and very alive during this last hour before sleep. Randal knew where his heroes walked, and leaning his tousled head against the fender, he wished them well and longed to be with them up there in that other land where he would be a hero too. He admired for a moment the silver hose and blue doublet of the Prince who awoke the Sleeping Beauty, and the ragged boy with a feather in his cap. Then he was in the Beanstalk with Jack, looking down on the gay procession, and mocking Goody Two-Shoes and Little Red Riding Hood, whom they both disliked. There Puss in Boots talked with Jack the Giant Killer, and in front of them was Beauty with her white arms round poor Beast's neck. And behind them all was the Dragon, whose grey length curved beyond the Giants and the blue forest, threading the hills like a road to the distant castle, aloof on its high crag. As the fire sank, lowering the shadows from the ceiling over Castle, Dragon and Giants, drawing Randal closer into its conspiracy, he forgot Jack and their bright morning in the Beanstalk, and returned to go through the forest with Hansel and Gretel, for they were his true friends; among the shadows and firelight of this timeless wonderland, he loved them more than his mother or even Katherine.

Sometimes, as he lay against the fender, snug in his woolly dressing-gown after his bath, he believed that he was really one of their company. The effort of make-believe vanished and he knew that he belonged to another world. It was a country of endless morning, of sailors and chests with seven locks and ships on the sea, and a white dusty road from the green sea and a tree which you could climb and watch the busy world of adventurers; and you could call out to them because they knew you and were always riding out quite near. Or, tired of the daylight, he could walk through the forest, where Hansel and Gretel took his hands and their eyes were blue as the magic lake and their hair was smooth and fair and they were lovelier than anyone else in the world. When Randal remembered these friends whom he had left for the world of his mother and Katherine, he wanted to die so that he could return to live with them always and never come back.

His relapse into this other life would be complete when Nurse had been reading to him. When Annie had cleared the tea things and drawn the curtains, Nurse would sit at the table with her hands flat on the thick cloth and say, 'Well, be sharp. Five minutes and then I'm off to get my sewing done. But I can't read the table-cloth.' So Randal would place his book open in front of her, and she would bustle over to the fire and settling herself in the carpet chair, she would read to him for a good hour. It was when she had finally closed the book and gone to get her sewing done that Randal would mount his rocking-horse and ride away, repeating aloud like incantations verses which he filled with allusions through which he rode into his wonderful country. His round dark eyes would shine entranced, his face flush and his hands lie cold on the bridle, as he chanted the magical lines:

'I saw a ship a-sailing,
    A-sailing on the sea;
And oh! it was all laden
    With pretty things for thee!

There were comfits in the cabin
    And apples in the hold,
The sails were all of silk
    And the masts were made of gold.'

When he had repeated this many times, his voice would fail at the line 'And oh! it was all laden,' and tears would try to spring in his eyes. Because everything in the world lay in the hold of the ship; but it had sailed away and he hadn't even been there to see it.

This song of regret had its counterpart in a song of proud possession. Then Randal would urge on his horse and draw tight the bridle. His eyes would glance about him in new bewilderment and he would cry out proudly to any dullard who might hear:

'I had a little nut-tree,
    Nothing would it bear
But a silver nutmeg
    And a golden pear.

The King of Spain's daughter
    Came to visit me,
All for the sake
    Of my little nut-tree.

I skipped over ocean,
    I danced over sea,
And all the birds in the air
    Couldn't catch me.'

He would shout this out, rocking rhythmically to and fro on his horse, plunging forward on the superb 'golden', falling away back on the

G. F. Green

breathless 'pear'. In an ecstasy of delight his spirit was stripped of
leaden body, and he was crazy with pride. For he held a secret talisman, a silver nutmeg or golden pear, something which gave him life
unimaginable to real people, where he was one of a brighter, happier,
more friendly company than those near him at home.

When Randal was nearly six, the Nurse left and he no longer quite
believed that Hansel and Gretel were truer than his sister Katherine.
He would still lean against the fender and mount his rocking-horse,
especially when he was disappointed by the real people, and dream
with the young princes and peasants in the shadows. But when he
was very unhappy, when Katherine and everyone hated him, then the
rocking-horse was silly and wooden and the frieze just pictures; then
he could no longer believe. But he would devote himself wholly to
Joseph, the living, black Labrador. He would pull him slowly towards
the fire, staring kindly into his brown eyes, then climb on to his back
with the rough fur warm against his bare knees and bury his face in
the rich darkness where the collar should have been. His hands, slipped
under the smooth flopping ears, closed against the long muzzle, and
lifting his feet, he crossed them over the back behind him. Then he
slid his hands forward over Joseph's eyes, and blind to the outside
world, they were one animal in the close blackness of the forest,
primeval and eternal. His whole body hugged the dog, moving before
the fire; became part of it like the muscles, and losing identity he lost
all attachments to reality. His responsibilities fell away. He relinquished
himself into another being, giving up all need to think or act or feel,
and insensible to all but the dark movement of which he was a part,
he enjoyed a sort of death.

Randal seemed to emerge from the lonely shadows of the nursery
into the chill light of day. His mother said, 'Katherine will soon be
going to school and I think it's high time Miss Andrewes turned her
attentions to you, young man.' So the nursery had a new table and a
Windsor chair. Miss Andrewes, the tall, beaded lady who knew so
much and was always going into rooms, shutting the door behind
her, now introduced Randal to a minor place in that serious and
learned conclave which formerly had separated Katherine and Katherine's governess from the rest of the household. The old nursery

had gone. The exercise books were shiny and new, and he only spoilt the difficult multi-lined copy-book. In the first weeks Randal smudged and blotted whilst Miss Andrewes corrected. But there came special afternoons when nothing seemed changed, remembered chiefly in the great days of summer or in November. Fog seemed to give cheer to the family at The Grange. When Mr Thane came in shuddering and stamping and muttering 'Rum weather for the convicts', for he was assured that far more escaped than we are told, Mrs Thane would draw the curtains with a shiver of relief, tell Randal to 'make up the fire for your father, dear, there's a good boy', and tea would be early and Annie would have made toast. The hours between tea and dinner, when the family were engrossed in his enormous jig-saw puzzle, *Nelson on the 'Victory'*, were as long and hot by the fire as on Christmas Eve.

It was on these afternoons, which Miss Andrewes called 'uninviting', that she would close her books earlier than usual, saying quietly to Katherine, as if they both knew very well what they were about, 'Well, I think that will do for to-day, and next Tuesday we'll get on to the aorist and perhaps learn some irregular verbs. Now let me see, what is the time?' She studied her wrist-watch, while Randal pretended to work gravely at his copy-book. 'Still another hour before tea.' Randal heard her words like a benediction. 'Then I think we'll get on with *Ivanhoe*; we haven't done any lately . . . Let me see, where had we got to?'

'Here, Miss Andrewes! It was Pax, then something in Latin . . . It was the password into the Castle and they told him he must—'

'Quietly, Randal; don't get so excited . . .'

'*Pax vobiscum*,' said Katherine; 'it's what friars have to say.'

'Yes, I remember . . . page 143. Now do sit still Randal and listen.'

'I am, Miss Andrewes.'

'Well, then.'

And so the wonderful tale would go on, all about Ivanhoe, the green woods, glossy black plumes and shining armour, the constant moonlit cells and the dazzling balconied world where pennons cracked white and blue, lances glittered amidst Kings and Princes, and the solitary Knight fell at the feet of his Lady.

The histories of Ivanhoe or Quentin Durward existed outside the nursery, and in his pursuit of these daytime lives he learnt more of the shrubberies, lawn and woods of The Grange. Growing older, it was here that he found a world enlarged from his books and dreams. Nursery fables Katherine had proved childish. A world founded among trees and shrubs was more durable and more credible, and Randal never doubted that its qualities arose from the very earth where he himself had stored them. Seeing the laurels' movement, he would feel their latent danger which if he were to doubt, he would be compelled to doubt the laurels too. It was only when he had rebuilt his world in a new symbol that he saw his delusion in the last.

The Grange was an old house. When Mr Thane had brought his wife to live there, he had planted near the front door a Virginia creeper which they both hoped would eventually cover the house beneath leaves larger than the ivy's. But the wind direct from the moor pinched its growth and Mr Thane still complained that it had not yet reached their bedroom window. 'I shan't be happy, Walters,' he would say, 'till I can lie in bed and see the leaves overhanging the window. It makes me feel as if the bedclothes weren't properly up to my chin. It makes me feel uncomfortable.'

All these years the house had never been redecorated and the uniform grey walls which were blotched with yellow gave The Grange a piebald look. It seemed to have grown along with the plantation, the large mottled lawn and the shrubberies, moist and evergreen reaching to the river.

The shrubberies were Randal's chief country of exploration; planted by Mr Thane to shut away the public footpath across the river, they were for Randal haunts of unknown extent. Here in a single morning, he might follow a strange trail, leading through dense thickets of berberis or holly or among glades of laurel and rhododendron, and all would be huge and gleaming as the forests of knights, medieval and forlorn. Here were always things to be achieved and discovered, and on rare adventurous days perhaps he might chance upon the clearing among the black-rooted laurels, which he had never found by searching. Then he would catch his breath and stare, leaning the gloomy leaves apart with his arms, for there were the chrysanthemums, bronze and white in their pale green stems, in sunlight recalling the chivalry of jousts and tourneys, or, under a dull sky, a company of knights and ladies, late beneath the castle walls. Believing that no one else knew of this place, he never mentioned his discovery. Amongst the shrubberies he enacted the adventures of Miss Andrewes' reading, more vigorous than the melancholy copse by the river. Randal rarely visited this wood, where the river showed through the trees like a vast white lake. For the stillness in the tangled brambles and the bare trunks of the trees was a relic of Hansel and Gretel, of ships which he had never seen, a power of transience and regret.

Though Randal was never allowed on the moor, unless Katherine went with him, he used to leave the garden and go inland through the village, up Church Lane harrowed by its black ogres. Once he had ventured beyond the church, where the two hillsides fell deep to a wooded clough. It was late afternoon. As he watched the other hill, it seemed to have a bare foreign look, and his face grew colder, thinking it might be Germany. It was deserted as if all the people had gone to be killed at the war. He began to feel strange, for the grass among the lost gravestones was much longer than at home, and he could not understand why there was no one about. It all seemed avoided as if nothing living ever came there. 'I wish I hadn't come,' he said, 'I wish Katherine was here.'

He was staring at a gravestone. There was the word 'YÉOMAN' carved on it. Randal went closer, the long grass covering his shoes. 'EDGAR LOCKHART', he read, then 'YÉOMAN', then 'DIED 12th October 1619', then 'GOD REST HIS SOUL'. Randal saw his breath through the chillness. He stared at the one word 'YÉOMAN'. He prayed for doubt, but none came to help him from his awful dread. He knew that the deadly word 'YÉOMAN' meant a man who had hanged himself for a sin. He knew that both sin and hanging doomed him unutterably below that one cold word. He knew that the deepest hell had buried him, leaving only the word to mean his crimes and torture, that in all the years perhaps no more than one had gone to hang himself in the night, so black in shame, Edgar Lockhart, yéoman. Randal stared at the word, holding his body full of the whole sin and death of Edgar Lockhart as he had glutted himself with the darkness of Joseph's animal movement. Until he shivered and drew back, glancing over the clough. Then he crossed himself in the silence there, as he had seen his mother do in church, and murmured from his lips, slow in the damp fog, 'God rest his soul'. Then he ran up the hill, past the church and all the way down the lane till he reached the village. And there he rejoiced in the lights from the butcher's and the sweet shop, and went home saying it was all over and he would never go there again.

But this power of evil fear was not lodged in the word on the tombstone. After the moment when it overcame him there, he knew that it haunted the shrubberies too. In his adventures he would suddenly long for the lighted drawing-room and run from the laurels believing that they darkened over him. Or, in the wood he grew anxious to be on the wide moor with Katherine. Soon, he came to realize that he alone was involved in these strange powers and would pass his days in a world far from the lunch-table life of his parents. Fleeing from the shrubberies he sought protection from a power which, unable to reveal, he could never escape, yet it was in these places that he sought shelter from unpleasant or dull reality. Mrs Thane observed how rarely Randal cried, unlike Katherine at his age. Instead of taking action against his trouble, like Katherine, until something was done, Randal used to wander through the shrubberies and down into the wood, forgetful of everything in an imagined world.

When Randal was seven Katherine left for school. 'And now,' said his mother, 'you'll be left in peace for a bit. Well, really, she'd begun to lead us all such a dance, it was time she went.' For the first day or two Randal, alone with Miss Andrewes, thought he agreed. But when every day began so far from bedtime; when they spoke less at lunch; when the hour before tea was just the clock ticking, Miss Andrewes turning a page or shifting a little when he purposely dropped his pencil; then he began to fret under the family peace. Soon there was no day when Randal failed to ask how long before Katherine came back. They became annoyed with him but he grew cunning, going one day to Miss Andrewes and the next to his mother, for although he might have remembered, he preferred to forget and ask again. Eventually, being afraid to ask any more, he made a list of days in his arithmetic book, crossing one off every morning as the nursery door shut behind Miss Andrewes. The last three days was a grabbing from meal to meal, like a desperate game of rounders, towards the base of Otterbourne Station. When he awoke early on the day, the sky was exciting in his window, far over the moor.

After breakfast, Randal set out with his father in the trap on the straight road across the moor to Otterbourne. He sat tight as wire, listening to the clattering hooves and the flight of the earth, as bewildering as his own wild mood. His big dark eyes narrowed in the joy of his musing. He felt his black hair driven in the wind like the plumes on the helmet of Ivanhoe. Astride a grey charger, he trampled the brilliant gorse under him, towards High Tor, where the blue-white radiance was like a veiled lady. He charged to the summit, declared conquest to the world of amber gorse – and suddenly all was Katherine. Beyond High Tor, he saw the railway sloping down to Otterbourne, and the roof and palings of the station. Knights and ladies had gone, exorcized by a more potent charm. In two minutes he would see Katherine. Terribly soon he would be near her laugh and the shake of her hand. Before was nothing; now was everything.

There was no need to tether the pony. In front of all her school things, piled against the railings, Katherine was waiting.

'Hello, Katherine.'

'Hello, Randal.'

Randal leapt down from the trap and seized his sister's hockey stick, instead of shaking hands. Katherine sat between them. Randal could hear his father telling her about Miss Andrewes' uncle who had given her a holiday at Bournemouth, how she needed it and how the sea air would do her good; then about the beech saplings which he had planted to hide the road, his mother's 'flu and how Uncle Armstrong and Aunt Grace were coming over for tea. The drive out had been a wild desire and battle, but the return was a calm triumph, full of good hope.

Lunch was like the first at the seaside when the sea-light fills the window with days of things to do in it. They all kept asking Katherine questions and she answered gaily, her voice alive with mockery. She imitated, Miss Blakiston, clipping on her pince-nez, and how once she had reported her for '"purposely colliding into me, Headmistress, when I was supervising the third side in Hockey" . . . she won't call herself a referee; why not?' Katherine munched lettuce leaf, eating along the stem like a rabbit.

'When does the aunt arrive, Mother?'

'They're supposed to be coming for tea, dear, but it's very trying because there are all your things to be unpacked and Annie has forgotten to put the valances on your bed; I asked her to be sure to have your bedroom done before they came, and then your Aunt Grace, though she is a relation of ours, and of course I'm not saying anything against her, naturally we're all very fond of her and pleased to have her—'

'—We'll be out,' Katherine said. 'Randal and me are going on the moor. Aren't we, Randal?'

'If you're going out, dear, I insist that you take your raincoats. It's very treacherous, the weather just now.'

'It's fine as Jupiter – Look.'

Randal saw and heard everything at this lunch. He watched the broken light in the salad bowl, the coruscating green Kia Ora bottle with its sunlit label, the cream cheese on a lettuce leaf specially for Katherine, and Katherine's quick hands dipping confidently into the salad bowl, and he felt in all this fresh light about the lunch and the new eagerness of his parents, a sense of bold life and of unquestionable authority. Now, for a month this certainty would be his.

As they were going out of the garden, 'Shove your coat,' Katherine said, 'under this old laurel. We don't want these things.'

'But what about Mother?'

'We'll get them when we come back.'

They set out towards High Tor. Katherine talked comically and scornfully about school. Randal learnt the truth about many things, and whenever she spoke with a slight toss of her head so that the fair hair was thrown back from the forehead, he knew the truth was not as he had thought.

'That Blakiston,' she said, 'sending us to bed without any supper.

I wish she'd go to bed and stay there. She's the sort that does eventually.'

Randal began to be tired by his continued laughter against the feeble enemies of his sister. He wanted to talk quietly with Katherine, without mocking people or laughing so much. He wished they were talking by the fire at home. But Katherine went on:

'She has what she calls her "quiet reading classes", and she reads Scott by the hour. As if anyone cared. And to hear her reading – I tell you who she's like.'

Randal frowned, his eyes gazing on the wide hostility of the moor. 'Miss Andrewes.'

It was as if a hawk had swooped on the cold expanse, out of which far away he heard Katherine's voice.

'—The way they talk, "Now dear, shall we do a little arithmetic?" I always wanted to say, "No, my good woman, we will not. You're sacked." Poor woman, she's all right. But she's past it.'

Randal stopped, stooping away from Katherine and held his ankle, pretending to feel for a stone in his shoe. The sense of venture caught from the certain, live Katherine at lunch was spoiled; he wished bitterly that she had never, never come back. In the sun, in the morning when their parents were busy, Katherine had been wholly right and he saw everything with her. Their wisdom was founded on a happiness whose nature was unguessed by their parents, shared through the confederate hours before tea when Miss Andrewes read to them by the nursery fire. He loved Miss Andrewes as something of the real world, which everyone else loved too, and more especially he and Katherine. She was unquestionable; to attack her was to break his whole established order. The protagonist whom he thought he had followed so safely had split open his round world. He felt laden with guilt on the darkening moor. He wished they had brought their raincoats.

'Let's go back,' he said, 'it's going to rain after all.'

Katherine tossed back her hair.

'Not yet,' she said. 'I know. We'll go to Otterbourne and have tea. We'll go back after the storm.'

Randal was afraid of Katherine as if she had been a stranger. He had never been so far on the moor but he dared not again ask to go back. As he walked beside her, he felt lost and submissive.

Through the tea-shop window they watched the rain sweep past High Tor.

'Katherine.'

'Yes?'

'What time is it?'

'Randal! I've only just told you; ten past five.'

'But it must be more. It was that last time.'

'Well I can't keep looking at my watch. I can't see what you want to know for.'

Randal wondered whether some interest which they had shared might remain whole, even now when all was shattered. He had to regain a small friendship where he would be safe temporarily, until he was again at The Grange before the log fire and the drawn curtains: all that this enemy had jeopardized; this bright and living enemy who had so nearly carried him away.

'Katherine.'

'What, Randal?'

'Do you think it'll rain to-morrow?'

'May.'

'Shall we do the birds' eggs if it does?'

'Yes, we might.'

'I've got two gulls' eggs now.'

'Gulls? Have you? I must see what I've got.'

'I'll give you mine,' he said.

With all his heart, he tried to recover something shared with Katherine, the fire and curtains which would shelter him from this foreign far-off tea-room, and give him confidence until he reached home and there would be no Katherine. In his simple treachery he forgot that the enemy returned with him.

When the rain had stopped they began walking back. The sky and moor had grown darker and as they walked the path showed white between banks of greyness. Their footsteps made clear alternating sounds. The rhythm of their footsteps and of the gathering night fascinated Randal like some reiteration in a dream, so that he felt alone, being guided unconsciously by Katherine. He seemed full of the dark rhythm, driving him from cold words, back to the warm and friendly talking, the old life. His mind, taut and blank to these last yards, waited for home.

'We left them here,' Katherine said.

The coats; they were of no importance now. Light from the french window was lying everywhere among the huge piled laurels, big with the storm which they had missed. They went into the light. He was nearly there, at the house. But Katherine had taken the coats and gone in. He was left where the wet-tongued laurels moved about their night business in front of an ugly congregation, spreading through slippery low arches, farther than any could guess, farther perhaps than the end of the moor. He knew that they were full of gathering danger, stilled only by the morning. He knew that he should be in the house, where his mother would have been since tea. He knew that they should never be out in the night. Then why did Katherine – but Katherine knew nothing of these necessities. He started to run to the house, when something thumped in his body. He stopped where the lawn opened black. Near the house, but out of the light, there were two people. They were big and dark; their movements were continuous and full of strange gestures; their low even talking gave them some fearful purpose. No one could be here in the night . . . Katherine would assume he knew. Katherine . . . even Katherine had gone in. The terror which he had warded off on the moor seized him. It was not the danger there by the house that beat in him but his knowledge of it, left here in the darkness, alone while the others were safely ignorant in the lighted rooms. He dared not move. He had to listen to their words.

The meaning grew with the realization of being familiar with the voices, so of their latent cruelty, of their direction against his house, of the two figures being Aunt Grace and Uncle Armstrong. They were speaking emphatically, their words rounded one after another like stones in a torrent. Randal heard their general purpose, broken by solitary words which jarred out from the rest, as a jagged rock might break up from the rough current. '*Suffocation*' surged up hungrily among their other words which were arguing against the warm room and his mother. Under the 'suffocation' their words hurried with terrible urgency as if preparing to destroy everything. He remembered that after his measles everything had been fumigated; the 'fumigation' had seemed just in time to prevent everything turning to deadly poison. Now he understood that '*suffocation*' had been discovered through and through his home. And then the word '*discipline*' broke through. It sounded harsh and keen, whilst their talking grew more angry. It tore at his mind like the red lashes in a sprain. It was this 'discipline' itself that was to kill his suffocating home. His terror had risen in their words like a wind to this climax, but now the word had fallen away; he was hearing them talk about Randal. He swallowed, breathing heavily, more complete and real fear. '. . . If this goes on much longer . . . it's high time someone took him in hand . . . It's time he went . . .' It's time he went . . . time he went, thought Randal. Just in time to be carried away by his uncle and aunt to a cold disciplined place, to be cleansed and cured from his life. And here, at The Grange, they would annihilate – everything. It's time he went . . . He shivered. Everything would be all right. It had to be. He would go into the house.

Then Aunt Grace spoke.

'Very soon, she'll have no child to spoil. Just look at the house. Look where Randal sleeps.'

Randal looked where Aunt Grace was pointing towards his window. He had always had a great affection for this window, the kindly face of his bedroom. It was hidden high under the roof, and everything about it was especially for him; the amount it was opened, the tin on the ledge, the yellow damp like a bear under the eaves; all these things were secrets between himself and his room, concerning no one else, part of a different life. Aunt Grace looked straight at his window, as if she would fetch out and destroy a thief. She began speaking again.

'No son of mine would sleep there, I can tell you. It's murder, Armstrong. Look at the angle of that chimney. It's leaning, with no kind of support, right over Randal's room. There's nothing to stop it. It would smash through the house like a bomb. It's murder to let that child sleep under it.'

Randal tilted his head back, staring in line with the pointing arm, where the roof was clean above the dark earth. Near him, the wind hurried the laurels. Aunt Grace's blouse grew uneasy about her arm. Then the chimney swayed . . . swayed high against the night clouds. It seemed to yield, indistinctly, like a cricket bat. Randal tightened every thread in his brain against the ending crash. He drew his skin close back to the face, his hands pressed like a clamp on his temples. He no longer heard the talk. The chimney swayed farther, gathering to its last pounding hurl against his home. His eyes were strained, his head crammed with the pain of the crash, increased as he tried to squeeze it back by pressing harder against his temples. He forgot Aunt Grace and the chimney and their talk. The pain released him from the nightmare where the lawn had been a black gulf, and now he ran across it towards the house.

Randal squeezed round the drawing-room door-knob, leant open the door, and clung to it arrested by the light and warmth. Everything looked blurred, and he waited. The people in the room shrank from the chillness in the open door, where the boy from outside stood white and faint, so that no one moved. Then his mother spoke.

'Randal dear, where have you been?'

She quickly crossed the room and lifted him in her arms. He found himself being carried in arms which he could hardly feel, through an Alice in Wonderland room with lights and looking-glasses and many people, smiling at him, proud of him. As if fading through the looking-glass he floated slowly away from the room.

He lay in bed in his clean flannel pyjamas, his straight black hair brushed smooth and his Jaeger dressing-gown buttoned to his neck. Against his head were the cool white mounds of pillow, and the eider-down covered his body like a country where his hands lay small and clear of his striped sleeves and far out of mind. He was liberated again to endless possibilities. He could be in a moment the Marquis of Stratford-on-Avon in the Blue Express to Vienna, at night to visit the Opera with La Somebody indiscreet and very famous, and by day to be diplomatic. Or he could – but his mother had taken the book from the table near the bed and was reading. 'Once upon a time there lived near a great forest a poor woodcutter with his wife and two children . . .' Randal closed his eyes. His fear was spent and he felt serious and loving. From over the snowy hills of pillow and the infinite tracts of eiderdown he could hear his mother reading, from a distant timeless land where he told this story of his own to himself and gradually began to sleep. His mother put down the book on the table.

'A chill,' she said, 'that's all.'

He just heard her. He frowned for a second, then turned away on his side, his hands across his face, and was asleep.

During the next four weeks Randal knew that there was a change in him, and he hated and denied it. There seemed no reason for the loss of his old unquestioning position, yet he could not regain it, and was most frustrated when he had spent the whole day with Katherine. Sometimes he surprised himself by a sudden image of his happiness before these holidays, when for a moment the garden was equal with Katherine and with either he could be happy. For now, he quarrelled often with Katherine and was bored if he was alone in the garden. He felt compelled to be where she was. He argued constantly against her, yet it was with her words that he set out to scorn his parents' opinions, failing, because he was trying to use the very words which he had striven to disbelieve. He seemed right only when setting out with nervous courage on these encounters with Katherine, which left him wretched and hating her. He was besieged and defending a Troy, driven to renew a contest which well might break up the walls and slit open the round towers.

So he fought for peace in arguments where the chances were loaded against some formerly safe opinion, whose destruction would leave him lost and afraid. Or he aimed at victory by expeditions over the fells which were farther than he was allowed to go, and ended in remorse. But there was no retreat. His task was to win himself this enemy's standpoint or prove himself at least in a pact. He tried to be her splendid equal, but always failed, for this combat was not for him, and he had to search then for his lost armour. So he hurried the days to Katherine's return to school. When he was rid of her, his faith in his spoiled world would return. There would be long truce. But the conflict had begun which would allow neither peace nor truce again.

The drive to Otterbourne meant little to Randal. He took no

interest in it nor in the thought of the train where they were to see Katherine go. He sat beside her, and behind them were all her school things. She had her overcoat on her lap because it was too warm to wear it, and he held the hockey stick between his knees. It was a fine day, but he did not look at the moor. He twirled the hockey stick between his bare knees and noticed each mark on the soiled plaster of the grip and minutely inspected the scratches on the yellow surface, thinking 'It'll soon have to be mended.' Then he laid it on its side and read the name of the maker, with the appearance of being an adept at the game. He closed his hands round the grip and used the heavy pole gently to move away the grit near his feet. He seemed absorbed in its least motion, looking at nothing else until they reached Otterbourne. He wished he played hockey. He wished he had a hockey stick worn and used like this one . . . yet at the same time he disliked it.

On the platform everyone was busy. Katherine was discussing things with her mother, and his father had gone to buy a paper. His mother looked round and said, 'It should be here soon.' Then the train appeared and came into the station. There was a hurried opening of doors and passengers getting into carriages which seemed already full. His father returned anxiously and the porter came with the luggage. He pushed it all into a compartment, under the seat or piled on top of other luggage, making room for Katherine. Randal laid the hockey stick, very light it seemed against the big suitcases, along the edge of the rack. Then he went out behind the porter, leaving the empty seat for Katherine, and she got in and shut the door. There was the last energetic talk with his parents and they stood back and consulted with the porter.

Now – burst on Randal's mind. *Now – Now – Now* – the climax of hidden thought struck his consciousness like a gong. He answered impatiently aside, 'I always do kiss her good-bye. Leave me alone.' *Now* – he jumped on to the step and the train started. He saw the light in her face, the last for an age. He kissed her mouth; found his eyes shut and opened them quickly to see her. The train gathered speed. *Randal.* 'Mother's calling me because the train's going and it's dangerous,' he thought. The palings blinked rapidly, blurred, and became a white wall. It took his breath. 'I'll be killed,' he thought. 'No. I'll only fall and be picked up.' He put his hand to her forehead so that the tips of his fingers entered the smooth hair, cold in the wind. 'Come back, Kit,' he whispered.

He jumped down to the rapidly moving platform, fell and got up quickly. 'Why ever did I say "come back"? Of course she'll – why . . . why did I call her "Kit"?' He blushed. The name filled him with possessive excitement, more even than his sister's actual presence. He repeated it in his mind, enjoying the surge of happiness at each repetition. The name was part of his last gesture: the fingers cold in the smooth hair as if dipped in a pail of water. He walked back down the platform, his body shaken by the fall, his mind entranced by his two expressions: Kit . . . the touch in his finger-tips.

'What possessed you to jump on to the train, Randal? Don't you know it's very dangerous? There was a man killed like that at Thursloe. Never do that again, do you hear?' Yes, he heard . . . for three months . . . thirteen weeks. Randal was back before the holidays, a child hearing the dull grown-up world surging back on him and the station gravel with its same dry crunch for each of their steps. He noticed that the gravel was a fainter colour near the palings. 'I suppose nobody walks so close, so it's left,' he thought, 'I might go and walk there. It's hardly worth it. It would mean walking extra, besides they'd all start talking to me . . . Kit . . . Kit it's all so awful now you've gone, and the same old hours with Miss Andrewes, and lunch . . . Oh what can I *do*?' Randal believed that he would weep, for every day would be miserable until Kit came back. For an instant 'Kit' and the chill in his finger-tips seemed to fly like a laugh through the weary talk of his parents crossing the station yard. But it passed and the gravel crunched at each lonely step and the palings moved by so slowly that he could see the long grey streaks where the paint had gone.

At lunch Randal ate silently. All liveliness had gone and it was as if the core of everyday life were dead, that had been dressed only in sham for visitors' sake. Kit, he knew now, was a visitor. He was one of the family, eating up the week's meals and bearing the pause of hours, until they were merged in the long baking and boiling of

Sunday, with church and thick suits, which Randal always associated with gluttony. His eyes wandered uneasily to the shut and locked french windows.

'Can I open the windows?' he said.

'Why can't you sit still, Randal? What's the matter with you to-day?' So the windows stayed locked until Kit came back.

Two days later Miss Andrewes, in her grey knitted dress over which fell her rope of bugle beads, with glossy black hat and shoes to match, paid the taxi from her worn purse, offered a threepenny bit and pulled the bell in the creeper by the front door of The Grange. With a general smile about the hall, ready, she unclasped her grey gloves as Mrs Thane approached from the stairs.

'A little rain,' she was saying, 'but nothing to trouble about. Randal caught a chill, just when Katherine returned, but I had no need of the doctor. And he's well now.'

'Where is he?'

Leaning over the banister, Randal saw Miss Andrewes arrive in the hall, grey and hung with beads as if harbouring pencils newly sharpened, and little red official boxes of nibs. He was glad to see her. He knew now that he longed to begin again. With relief he felt the whole excitement of getting things out and arranging and talking and of her kind leisurely voice folding him away and back, as a bee lost to the world is enfolded by the closing petals of a flower. He shook her hand, and her frail woollen texture with its odd jingle and her patient instructive smile, gathered him into her domain. Content, he watched her going to her room, followed by her boxes.

In the morning there was a fire in the nursery and two chairs at the table. Once more, Randal and Miss Andrewes worked together, uninterrupted. Soon Miss Andrewes' holiday was forgotten, nobody thought of Kit, and Randal was plunging through the shrubberies to follow the strange ways of the Cat that Walked by Himself, or extending the lawn to a sunswept desert and leaping on and on in the heat, full chase after Yellow-Dog Dingo. But Randal and his world had changed. Kit had gone, Miss Andrewes was back, but when he returned to the shrubbery, he found it altered; he was conscious of the make-believe. He lost its sure reality, and at times he deliberately embroidered it. His pleasure did not waver but it became less serious. He roamed the garden in a more cavalier spirit, ready to tilt at a giant for the fun of proving it a windmill. Sometimes he shocked Miss Andrewes and himself too by this scepticism.

One morning she came into the nursery to find the fire crackling under a log and the window smudged by snowflakes. 'Santa Claus will soon be here!' she said. 'Then they'd better put off the sweep,' he replied. But he hated the logic of his words and tried despite everything to disown them.

His imaginary world now failed as a talisman, and he no longer visited the wood. The powers, once so real to him and incomprehensible to the others, had become insufficient in face of trouble, which too was now more urgent. He began to suspect that they held some more potent talisman than he against evil and difficulty. So one day he said, 'How do you stop things happening to you, you don't like?' and his mother answered, 'By prayer, dear. We pray.'

That afternoon Miss Andrewes came into the nursery, not looking at all well, Randal thought. She told him to put away his books for he would not be needing them this afternoon. Then she sat down by the fire and opened a black book, with an aggrieved air and little subdued coughs, so that her beads jingled whenever she lifted her tired hand before her mouth. She said:

'Sit down, Randal, and listen carefully. I've something to tell you.'

Miss Andrewes read from her black book, in a voice full of grief, which made the clock tick louder than ever before. There were odd phrases which he liked and kept repeating in the various rhythms of the clock; 'And it came to pass' was one, 'Verily I say unto you' was another. But after some time, Randal grew sorrowful because Miss Andrewes was so sad and because he thought that perhaps she would never again read the *Just So Stories*. 'I won't want any tea,' he thought.

Suddenly she closed the book and said, 'I think you would understand better if I told you in my own words.' Then she smiled and everything seemed as it used to be and she told about a beggar who travelled all over the world, telling such wonderful stories that everyone stopped working and followed him to hear more. Miss Andrewes told him some of them. 'But of course,' she said, 'my words are less than shadows of His' (he had never heard her talk so oddly). The one he liked more than all the rest was about a Sultan from Arabia who grew forests from grains of mustard seed, and when he went to war, hurled whole mountains on to the enemy's ships. After this story, Miss Andrewes had turned to him with a blissful smile, saying very quietly, 'And you or I could do the same, Randal, if we only believe.'

For some time Randal ceased to listen. Then, overwhelmingly, he said: 'Miss Andrewes.' He was going to be very clear and explicit. 'Why don't people pray that the war will end? Because if they did God would stop it.' And Miss Andrewes who remembered that she had a nephew at the Front (indeed how could she ever forget?) answered with resignation, 'They do pray, Randal. But there is too little faith in us. Could we only believe in our dear Lord, He would hear . . . He would grant our prayers; for we are praying for the lives of His dear ones and for the overthrow of His enemies.'

Randal knew that this was beyond his understanding. 'The truth is, they don't know the word,' he decided. 'It's been forgotten since the Arabian Sultan had it.' And he wondered whether it would ever be discovered again.

Randal's birthday was on a Monday. He would be eight. The promise they had given him was a day's drive over the moors. Constantly he saw the trap, its wheels spick and span and its wicker luncheon basket closed, unrifled. Like the day's chrysalis it held strange tors, lanes and streams unexplored, and especially the unbroached fact – eight, to be celebrated and unravelled throughout the day. The yellow trap, packed still and tight in the greenish mist, was like a filbert among its leaves within hand's reach, ready to be split between the teeth. Randal kept the idea of his birthday as a possession, sacrosanct and intact. He thus avoided all the suspense of looking forward to an actual day.

But the Sunday aroused his eagerness and anxieties. He remembered fearfully his mother's warning, 'If it rains of course, we can't go.' The sky seemed veiled with malignant clouds, the laurels were moist and dull, the whole day was sultry with intention to spoil. Before, he would have exorcized this through his mind's more real adventures whilst the rain spoilt his day. But now he was impatient.

Like the hot scratching at a nettle-rash, his desire for this trip recurred. All that Sunday he sought for a solution.

After tea Mr and Mrs Thane went with Randal to church. During the week the church had few visitors, but its pews and brasses were steadily polished and its stoves heaped up, till it burgeoned among its pealing bells, rich in comfort, engendered in its wreaths of incense and warm pipes coiling from subterranean boilers. Mr Hayton, the rector, moved quietly about the building in his thick cassock and slippers, with the assurance that his church was warmer and more habitable than many homes. Randal released his thoughts to pasture like cows in summer, amongst the warm smells of incense, hot pipes, polish and gas or to flutter like moths around the gleam of memorial tablets or the long chains and lamp up above; or even like butterflies to dazzle amidst the constellation about the altar, the alabaster towers of candles, the creamy mouths of the gladioli, lost in a celestial brilliance.

Here he watched Mr Hayton lead his choir-boys, and it was as if in this procession he witnessed the gradual approach of his eighth birthday. Immediately all became anxiety. The progress of the service was marked now by its units, a hymn or Mr Hayton's chubby hand turning a page, things that had to be finished and checked, like a list of school things before he could go. It became increasingly involved arithmetic. He counted the hymns, psalms and chunks of prayer which remained, adding 'then supper, then bed, then to-morrow'. He reckoned the verses of hymns and psalms, estimated the length of the sermon in minutes, reducing it with difficulty to seconds, and even counted the choir-boys before he remembered that they had no influence on the duration of the service. Through these calculations his eyes fixed on various bright objects, as if they were parts of to-morrow. Whilst he seemed to devour one, he was driven to scrutinize another, each tense and thrilling with its quality of desire. Thus he tried to catch a certain voice which floated in clarity above the rest of the choir, the circlet of precious stones in the cross on the altar, the meaning in a line of hymn, and was striving to comprehend the flimsy surplice, the preoccupied face, with the fair hair brushed away from the candlelight, of the choir-boy whither he had traced the solitary voice, when Mr Hayton's announcement 'Psalm an hundred

and thirty-nine . . . Psalm one hundred and thirty-nine', recalled him
to the more urgent work of calculation.

He turned to his psalter. Twenty-four verses. Twelve each side,
then the bit at the end, then the lesson, then more psalm, then another
lesson, then . . .

'If I say Peradventure the darkness shall cover me, then shall my
night be turned to day.'

Randal did not hear the singing. He read the sentence again:

*If I say Peradventure – the darkness shall cover me – then shall my night
– be turned to day.*

Excitement beat inside him. He was seized with its meaning. *Peradventure – night – day*. Darkness – *Presto* – Light. It is night
– *Peradventure* – it is day. He had discovered the word.

There stood the Arabian Sultan calling 'Peradventure!' to fields of
mustard and lo! they were forest, shouting 'Peradventure!' to the
mountains and like worlds they fell on the enemies' ships. *'Peradventure!'* He stood on the summit of Mount Everest with sword of
tempered ice, commanding the world, a prince in miraculous armour!

Randal forced calmness on to this outburst of triumph. For centur-
ies they had missed the hidden word and children had never bothered
to attend. Now he had discovered it . . . found it by chance, 'Peradventure', right in the middle of a psalm. And now he would use it
secretly. His calculations were over. He smiled at the ignorance of Mr
Hayton and took pleasure in the voice of the choir-boy, in a region
remote from anxiety.

In his bedroom, Randal watched his bed with the chequered counterpane spread under the light, and because he felt so dramatic, a
sense of possession goaded his delight in the soft colours. Like his
father washing his hands in cold water before a committee meeting,
he scoured his teeth and rinsed his face with rapid importance, aware
of his autobiography. Then he knelt, feigning indifference, beside his
bed and pressed his elbows into the yielding counterpane. Usually
this moment merely concealed the exploration of his face where he
would run his finger-tips easily along the smooth contours, tracing
the circles of his eyes, the line of his nose and the bracket of his
mouth, ending by rippling them through his hair as if they were not

his own. To-night his hands and face were taut like sculpture, and his prayers rapid. They stopped. He shut his eyes into a tight darkness. He took a dry empty breath and, as if reading out the correct answer of a sum, he spoke aloud.

'Peradventure, God . . . *Peradventure* it will *not* rain to-morrow. Amen.'

Then he pulled back the counterpane because he felt so hot and got into bed.

In the morning Randal awoke early, feeling eight. For a moment he lay still. He sat up, keeping his eyes shut and then he opened them, suddenly, full at the window. It was pouring with rain. The cold panes throbbed in the rain like a sullen duckpond. The rain streamed down them blearing the flat dawn. The columns of rain collapsed on the window-sill loudly, almost inside the room. Randal sat watching it, wishing it would stop, but it didn't stop. Deliberate and impersonal, as the laurels had seemed that far-off night, with unalterable motion the rain fell, mile upon mile, over the grey marshy land. Randal lay down again and pulled the warm bedclothes over his head. 'O God,' he protested silently.

He began to comfort himself, holding his shoulders with his crossed hands, persuasive like a friend. But at last he grew ashamed and through the grey deluge of rain came the recollection of tall Aunt Grace in her grey costume, speaking to his mother: 'Not all of us joyride every day. Armstrong has an important meeting. We must decline.' An occasion long ago, when they had taken their drive over the moor, and because of Aunt Grace's refusal, he had been oppressed with guilt all day, as if their pleasure lessened someone else's store. The rain and Aunt Grace were important, not his own fears and outings. He was wrong to dread them, ashamed of his belief in God, for not even Miss Andrewes would dream that he could have been so weak as to take it seriously. Bitterly he repudiated all his imaginary powers of the nursery and the garden, which no ordinary boy would have believed. 'It's a lie,' he cried, 'it doesn't work . . . none of it.' Yet only he was helpless, whilst Aunt Grace and the outside world lived untroubled without God or stories. All his life he must conceal this sin, his hopeless beliefs and love of joy.

Randal lay exhausted in the grey world, hearing the rapid energies of the rain swilling the roof, clearing the panes, gurgling along the pipes, threshing the miles of resistant heather and forcing the brooks into heavy gluttonies, and it seemed to him that the world would overwhelm him. He closed his eyes and pretended to sleep. More and more hours with Miss Andrewes fell away before him . . . they would never quite reach the end of the month; something came to stop them. He awoke to think it out. Kit returned. Kit came back on Friday. That was it – Kit and walks on the moor. Randal stirred. There was Kit to be considered. Did anything matter, when Kit came back? Kit, there always, Kit with her hair thrown back, her eyes chiefly for him, her quick beautiful hands, which would often, all through his life, touch him?

Like laughter the realization filled his body that he was above them all. He had a power of his own and could scorn them. He believed beyond life in Kit. 'I'll do everything for her,' he said, 'and I don't care if she dislikes me, I'll just go on doing things for her.' The greyness had vanished from his world it seemed for ever, since there existed indefinitely a love which demanded no return. In place of those images which had once secured him, was the one image of a girl, whose words were like bright metal, whose thought drove daringly, whose life wherever it may be, was the one thing real. In this great image he held the unique talisman. And now Randal knew no more the magic securities of childhood, learning his sentence of perpetual dependence on another, to whom his renunciation would mean nothing, and he entered gladly the prison of another's life.

On Friday morning, Mr Thane tapped the barometer in the hall, which trembled to 'Very Fair'. 'That means it will be fine driving,' he said. 'That's a good thing.' Randal stood in front of the dining-room fire waiting for breakfast. He was still fresh from his bath and he felt very neat and handsome. His hair was newly brushed. He had put on a clean jersey and stockings, which held him tight, and he was very proud of his hands, placed deliberately across his belt, so that they seemed to follow the line of a doublet. His legs astride, bent slightly back, and his arms akimbo, he needed only an audience.

Miss Andrewes went into the nursery. She collected her books, putting them on the middle shelf of the bookcase whence they could be moved without disorder; then she sat unsmiling in the sunlight at the end of the long table, with a list of her books, many times checked and folded, before her. As she glanced in the quiet room from the books to her list she remembered the companionship of the hand-some dark-eyed child to whom she had given happiness, hidden in her readings from exactly chosen tales where her care had been to understand the least tremor of his mood, even to draw the curtains at the right pause in the story, to call cheerfully for tea at the resolu-tion of adventure, to kindle this nascent and sensitive imagination. To-day all this would end. And she remembered with regret those moments when, with a sudden intuition, he had turned to her in bewilderment, his face wonderful in the firelight, and she had faltered, refrained, and concealed the truth of her gift. Since her return she had watched his faith waver and a new restlessness usurp him, had known its climax to be this day. Afraid, she had ceased to read to him. For she knew that he could never forgo the illusion of safety, which she had given him, to go unprotected in the world.

When a girl, she had possessed a love bird. One day her nervous fingers had let the gate of its cage spring open and her bird had flut-tered pitifully about the strange room. Afraid to catch it and restore it to its cage, she had excused herself by saying, 'It is too late now. It has been free and would pine to be shut up again.' So she had opened the windows and the bird had flown out into the garden. Next day, the gardener had brought her the dead bird. 'You'd have done better to have kept it in its cage, missie,' he had said. 'It wasn't accustomed to the cold and having to forage for itself. It would get weak and the spadgers would kill it.' Now she heard again that same frightening beat of wings as she continued to check her books.

'Morning, Miss Andrewes.'

She looked round at Randal, wild and excited.

'Good morning, Randal.'

'Isn't it a marvellous day? And, Miss Andrewes, I've got my Cor-onation mug. I can keep it now. The one with crests and crowns and flags and cornets all over it—'

'Coronets, you mean.'

'—Cornets and the King and Queen. We're going to have early lunch. What shall I do this morning?'

'I've some things I must do before lunch. I think you'd better finish learning *The Miller of Dee*.'

'Look, Miss Andrewes, there's a hawk.'

'Yes, but come away from the window. Randal, sit down now. It's time you began.'

'It's a kestrel. Look, it's hovering.'

'Randal, do you hear me?'

'It's swooping. O the wings! I'd love to be a kestrel. It looks rusty from the rain.'

'Randal, for the last time, sit down. Please get on with your work. There's a lot to be done this morning.'

Randal sat down and opened his book, but not in obedience, merely that he was ready to start. The beginning of the morning passed. The hours filled out and turned smoothly on whilst into the silence which lay between the governess and the boy the fire shifted, easing itself, a coal fell into the grate, or a stick crackled. At times the window drummed briefly. Whilst the last hour went by, Randal kept glancing up.

'I've learnt it. Shall I say it?'

'Soon, Randal. Make sure you know it properly.'

She regretted these disturbances which made her conscious of the two of them sitting at one end of the long table. She began to feel constrained, even shy towards this boy whom she would betray. As twelve struck from the hall, she gathered up her pencils, her box of nibs, her indiarubber and her pen, and put them back into her black oilskin bag. This then was the end. She spoke reassuringly.

'Now, Randal,' she said.

Randal jumped up and stood at the farther end of the table by the window. He began:

'*The Miller of Dee*.
There was a jolly miller
Lived on the river Dee.
He wrought and sang from morn till night,

No lark so blithe as he.
And this the burden of his song
For ever used to be,
"I care for nobody, no, not I,
If nobody cares for me.""

He recited well in a clear, gay voice. Miss Andrewes postponed her thoughts, allowing the boy and his poem to be enough and without sequel.

At the second stanza a noise hurried and jarred to a standstill at the window. They looked and all seemed in disorder. Kit on a bicycle with her foot on the sill and the wind in her skirt and her hair flying and her eyes bright in the wind; Kit was laughing in at the window. Miss Andrewes had the impression that the walls of the room had broken, and their quiet shared personality fled. She saw Randal's face flush like a lover's. For an instant she thought he would ignore her and run from the room. Quietly she checked him.

'Continue, Randal. Finish it.'

He went on reciting, but in an unnatural strident voice no longer caring.

'Slower, Randal. Attend to the words.'

But she saw him smiling at Kit, smiling back.

'Randal, speak slowly. Not so loud.'

He deliberately heightened the tone. Faster, louder, and with wild affectation, he flung the words to the room whilst he moved his lips for Kit.

'No lawyer, surgeon or doctor
E'er had a groat from me,
And I care for nobody no not I,
If nobody cares for me.'

He sang out the refrain with impossible mockery.

'Randal!'

She must hold him to the words till the poem was done. If only she could keep him with her to finish this last lesson together. He was laughing, with his sister's encouragement as he recited the last stanza. It was too much. She would have to stop him, yet if they could but reach the end—

'Randal, please do it properly. Then you may go.'

She heard the boy answering her louder than ever, louder than could be borne.

'The song shall pass from me to thee.'

Her last whisper of his name was unheard as he yelled at her in the room, with his face triumphant towards Kit.

'And all in heart and voice agree
To sing "Long live the King".'

'That's enough. All right. You may go.'

Not listening to what she said but as if acting on his own impulse Randal ran from the room, whence his thoughts had long since fled. Kit also pushed off from the window-sill and bicycled from sight. Miss Andrewes waited alone for a moment in that useless room where she heard only the coals shift in the fire. Then she shut the nursery door and crossed the hall to the drawing-room. Mrs Thane was alone, arranging a flower bowl on the piano.

'I would like to speak to you about Randal,' Miss Andrewes said, 'before lunch if I may. It's important.'

It was this conversation between them which decided that Randal must be sent to school.

PART TWO

The Truth Game

Randal sat down again in the corner of the sofa beside Bourne. His face flushed gloriously amongst the confusion of the fire's heat and the light shadowed by laughing boys which glutted the full room to the heavy curtained windows. The pieces of furniture and each of the boys were eclipsed by a blissful triumph like a dream. He had tightened his wits to win this first difficult position, where he handled his story lightly to divert their sting, then easily completed it, assured of their good humour. And now these boys in whose power he was, were like dogs fawning for more. Randal was ten and old enough to know where he stood among the clever and the mighty, so he was silent and smiled.

The pleasure of how he had told his story lay complete in his head while his face was blushing at their cries for more, as a cloud of lit smoke hangs ample over the hurrying carriages long after the engine has brought it forth. Bayliss was his herald. As soon as Dagan's geography lesson was over, Bayliss ran exciting with the news that Thane had a special Dago story. 'Thanery must tell it,' he said. 'He's marvellous on Dago.' Despite their mistrust of this Bayliss gang, the boys in the Green Room had hurried away from tea, to be in time. 'There's nothing to tell,' Randal began. And thence he had expanded, exaggerating richer tales of famous jokes, creating a Dago saga where he himself was Dago. They roared with laughter and he yelled straight at them, scared, Dago's great shout: 'Shut y'r row!' Their laughter burst over him for more. Released amid this gutted danger Randal smiled. It was that shout and the point where he stood up before the fire, which he most enjoyed.

He had familiarized himself with the least inflections of his story which he now explored again, but his ardour died. He was faced with the event from which it had arisen. The continual fears of his two years at school fell chill through his body. The background of vacant classrooms and boys in the daytime laid bare the incidents of this lesson. During the morning he had dreaded it. When it began, he sat gripping his book, his face set white. The boys answering weighed on his own ignorance; each right answer a dead load. Then his turn came and the feeling of being stunned by Dagan and his class.

'Thane. What is the chief industry of Lancashire?' His head minute, his ears blocked, he was sure that he neither heard nor might answer correctly. The question was simple and they smiled in league with Dago.

He stared at the ceiling till his stretched throat made his eyes ache. Any inkling of geography was denied him. Then suddenly Dago's grey face came close to his.

'It's no use looking up to Heaven, child. You'll get no help from there.'

Loud came their shattering laughter. They screamed like a racing car while he waited, and finally said 'Wool,' slipping it into the din where he hoped it would mingle away, leaving the next boy to answer.

'Shut y'r row!'

The noise ended.

'What lies are you telling me, Thane?'

Because he must say something and because they had been laughing Randal said,

'That the chief industry of Lancashire is wool.'

Then it was all over.

'Child, you should be thrashed – next!'

When Randal put away his books he was shivering and the hair at his temples was still rough. The tea and thick bread-and-butter warmed him. He looked round and wondered at Bayliss chattering gaily, his curly head swirling about like a brandished doll, spreading the news that Dago had been mocking God. Over the table, round behind him, eagerly across his neighbours, 'Thanery must tell it,' he explained. 'After tea in the Green Room.' Everyone knew that Dago was an atheist and never nodded his head in the Creed. It was a good story Randal thought, and he was pleased that he liked Bayliss. He could certainly do the remark about Heaven especially when he had peered at him, and he would include the way he stalked into chapel and turned his back on the altar . . . They clamoured for that again. But he enjoyed their company round him even more than their laughter.

They were all quieter now, leaving him alone. Several were persuading Hayley to tell one of his ghost stories and someone had turned out the light. Randal saw them more clearly as they settled round the fire. He felt an untroubled friendliness towards them. Then Bayliss, who was on the floor, leaning against the sofa, looked up and Randal was aware only of him, because his hair and upturned face seemed nearer than everything else. He looked at Randal as if no one else were there and said, pleading confidentially, 'Thanery, go on. Tell us something more.' Randal was incapable of answering. He felt like one laughing stopped by something serious. He felt restless. His feelings came to an end and broke back to his first night at school where another gesture had provoked an equivocal response and could not be explained.

That first memory, after the visit to the headmaster and to the matron in the Linen Room, was a fantasy of wandering through multitudinous corridors, flights of unending stairs, rooms with vast darkening windows, through a country of light and darkness, of nightmare. He was lost, searching again for the white door of the Study or the Linen Room which was busy in a passage of many lights. In the midst of this labyrinth was a vast cold hall circled by galleries. As its dome became greyer his eyes ached staring down at the lines on the tiled floor, whilst in the height of its round walls, through the square openings of the corridors, it was clear of sound and people. His search must have been forgotten for he had wandered along, his fingers touching the straight walls until he had emerged into a large square of light. He was looking into a room crowded with boys and out of the jumbled light and noise a voice leapt at him.

He could think about this more definitely because he now knew the facts as they had happened. Mole had asked him what he called himself. He had said 'Randal Thane'. Then they laughed and Mole jeered at him and he had gone to the back of the room where he had met Bourne. But after that, the confusion began which he could not unravel. They were shouting and climbing over the desks, and he stood beside Bourne at the back, when a boy came to the door from outside and they all turned and welcomed him. They kept shouting his name and they seemed filled with a wild delight.

Randal tried to see Felton in the doorway, missing out the last two years, as he had been that first night. But the irritation which centred on him had only increased. Why should he be different? Determined, Randal forced himself to see Felton stand smiling again in the doorway. He was dressed differently. He had his handkerchief in the breast pocket of his red blazer, and the white collar of his shirt turned up, and his white shorts tightly belted clear of his knees – but it was not his clothes. It was his look which was conceited. His face had the light and bragging air of the seaside and his blue eyes were cold and scornful. He came in and ignored everyone except Mole and Colshaw. Randal saw again this strange indifference. How could such conceit make him liked? He never ceased to fear and loathe Mole and Colshaw and Felton. He never understood whether he hated them all or one of them particularly, or whether this tireless frustration could only be hate. Felton had turned from the crowd and sat on a desk near the door. Then he looked across at Colshaw to the back of the room and for an instant his eyes met Randal's. He could not answer the look and turned to Bourne with a more subtle disturbance than the fear of that first night.

In the morning he awoke to the new building. He began meeting the boys and fitting their names, and the terms had begun. The school, high in the hills, commanded the lesser hills and valleys which fell towards the Bristol Channel. It faced across a road which was divided by a white painted railing from a broad grass terrace with a white mast in the centre. From the mast a scarlet-bordered Union Jack cracked in the winds as if straining at a leash. Over the plunge of hills from the sea the west wind blew flat at the many windows. The building was long and white and its roof was of red pantiles. The mast, the rows of bare windows, the terrace like a quarter-deck and the white rails, were bright and shipshape as a yacht spanking along in a fair breeze or even a well-kept battleship. The tiled length of a corridor ran from end to end of the building, opening out where the Lobby was a whirl of light below its shining glass dome and tiered galleries. Like the classrooms, the corridors had cream-coloured boards divided by a red strip from the wall above. 'Every line and colour,' said Mr Western, the headmaster, 'is designed for young life.' From the Lobby, doors led to the Changing Room, the Big School, the terrace and, farther on, to the Green Room.

Randal soon learned his way in these surroundings. Always with the mild Bourne at his side, he formed a habit which sheltered him from contact, as rigid as law or fortifications. Before lunch the landing by the Dining Hall was to be avoided, for it was then that the talk was dangerous, but before tea its character changed and there was much to say to friends. The Big School had seven lofty windows, all uncurtained and open, and at the far end was a piano and a tall desk. Above the red strip on the white wall hung a bright portrait of Charles II; facing it across the rows of desks was a more sober portrait of Oliver Cromwell. The Big School was never to be visited. But the far end of the passage, where the hot pipes were and a small window looked south, was deserted and warm and smelt of old books. Here he often came. Outside, at the North End of the terrace the Colshaw gang kicked footballs, but on the earth slope under the Common Room he enacted the drama where Hayley's racing car crashed over precipices, Hilton was shot dead by the rebel Toone and Bayliss gunned his way out to the hostage in his cell, behind the garden gate.

Two years had made his position safe among the boys who frequented the Green Room, and the success of his stories had spread and he ventured farther. There were mornings when he was no longer at the South End. He moved about the long terrace during the break talking to masters or groups of boys whom he knew less, creating his role of mimic. Dago himself or the other masters listened. Little Willie who had visited Toledo in his youth called him Greco because of his pale face, his black hair with the red gleam of a newly shelled chestnut, his large and dark eyes and his hands with the chill neat fingers. 'Like an El Greco donor,' he mused. Dago laughed. 'See him frightened. He's like the child of Russian refugees.' As Randal talked and acted among friends, he knew that Harding and Felton, practising at the North End, had paused for an instant, disarmed, to watch.

As Randal was rarely absent from the South End during the break or after tea in the Green Room, so he was always with Bourne who was the chief part of his habit. When there was a walk on the hills or plain they went together, and on free afternoons they sat under the Great Elm, at the top of the sloping Paddock, and watched. Below them were scattered the huts where boys kept their pets, and beyond the village path Felton and his helpers were busy in 'Hentown' constructing new houses for his fowls. Far beyond, the country stretched to the sea and they would ask each other again what the shining thing in the distance could be, which never altered.

But these years seemed more of the winter and it was not until his second summer that Randal had emerged.

Now as he sat beside Bourne, with Bayliss near him on the floor, he considered everything which had changed since that strange night when Felton had first seen him and he had been lost in the labyrinth of corridors. He knew again the seclusion of Miss Graves's classroom where there had been drawing lessons and map colouring, and later the third form where sometimes Little Willie had enlivened his history lesson by his famous representation of Horatius Keeping the Bridge, with the black-board ruler wavering against his thin comic shadow. He remembered each of his friends and their adventures, as if he were leaving them behind in the morning.

For the sofa seemed to carry him away. These impressions had gathered in the Green Room where none were above the third form and there had always been shelter. Here he would transform as if by magic into laughter and warmth those events which had terrified him in the daytime. Under the iron arch the fire enriched the darkness where they sat on the floor before the thick green curtains. He had rushed to the sofa, taken possession and lay now secure in his corner. Across the fire Hayley told a ghost story. Randal followed it through the folds of country which was Bayliss's hair, burnished in the stream of firelight and amidst the shadowy toasting forks which two boys turned inspecting their toast, and to-morrow seemed there for ever until the steps and shouts struck along the tiled passage outside.

*

Randal's dislike of Rugger increased where no part of the skill of his body could yet be shown. On one of the afternoons towards the end of the term there was the usual game under a sky pinched bleak with wind. Randal hated it. He stood about the field, disinterested, flapping his arms against himself and hardly knew which side he was on. Marsden, dodging a tackle, tripped over him and shouted at him. He shivered angrily only to feel, alone again on the field, that Marsden was right. Finally the whistle blew. Dumb to relief, he fetched his spare jersey and joined Bourne walking close to the fence. He pulled down his sleeve over his hand and shoved open the gate, wet and icy, leaving the churned fields behind. They hurried up the road to the school, wretched but for the steaming baths there, and were in the steep lane when Randal began to drop behind. The voices and brisk steps of the first game kicked and shouted about him. He hurried through the leaves, trying to overtake Bourne. Mole was on his right, and looking round at him. He felt his eyes fix on his clean shorts as Colshaw ran up to him.

'Afraid the mud might hurt you? I bet you can run. Run then.'

Colshaw's red, dark face stared with hatred into his.

'Can't even run, look!'

Felton, his hands in his pockets, his shoulders swinging forward, was kicking a stone up the hill. He looked down at the road so that his hair, fair as Kit's, hung in front of his eyes. He kicked the stone scuttling along the road, threw back his head, clearing his wide blue eyes to the sky and called out mockingly:

'No one's taught him!'

Mole had a graze of mud across his narrow forehead. Colshaw's jersey, shorts and stockings were a wall of caked mud. Close round him they hurried among the leaves where up the road Felton still kicked the stone. Randal was far behind them. He knew that Felton wasn't covered in mud. He had seen that his shorts and red jersey were clean, that his wrist, between the shrunk sleeve and the edge of his pocket, was clean. He was annoyed, not afraid. Didn't Felton know that you were a bad player and a shirker if you were clean? That he had no right to be thought good and in the XV? That he had no right to be the equal of Mole and Colshaw? They at least were covered in mud. Randal tried again to see Felton in his mind. His every conceited movement spoiled the proof of his unsoiled clothes, and this confused vision angered and frustrated him, cheating him of evidence. He longed to justify to himself that Felton should be ashamed. Mole and Colshaw were obviously disagreeable and their unpopularity was assured, but Felton – it was Felton he wished to denounce. He climbed the road to Bourne and they came up with the others. He thought only of Felton, his shrunk red jersey, his hands in the pockets of his shorts, the swing of his shoulders, his kicking the stone, the toss of his head and mocking laugh. It proved nothing. He longed to smash his pose, to argue about him, make him see, make everyone see how wrong they were to like him.

The bathroom steamed with yellow light whose warmth Randal felt about him while he flapped the great towel quietly over himself. He fastened the silver snake in his red belt firmly between the white flannel of his shirt and shorts, raised himself on his stockinged feet and brushed his hair solemnly before his flushed face in the glass. There were lights in the passages, and work would soon begin, and his body was too tired for anger, tranquil to the shame that he had felt outside which merged with the autumnal pleasure of the hot bath, and lingered beneath his careful clothes. His seriousness lay in his pose, his pre-occupied ways, for he was wholly conscious of himself. He walked along the passage to the Big School, where he read the Time Table – Dago's Latin. He could no longer dread it. He was tired of being afraid, the schemes and tricks during the game, the pretence of tackling, the false fall, even the glancing down at the fake nail in his boot. This meanness wearied him, going on perhaps indefinitely, avoiding everyone like Felton, who despised him. What possibly could Felton see to like in Mole and Colshaw? He was the best player in the XV, the best in everything. No one on earth could equal Felton.

The form was working in silence over their Latin word lists. When Dago had entered the room he had said, 'This afternoon you can revise your word lists. And I don't want a sound. If anyone talks he'll be thrashed.' Since then he had sat like a grim idol at his desk, correcting. The relief from fear, the contentment of the form with nothing before them until tea, gave his thoughts ease to bourgeon. He became engrossed in them for they had never before been so coherent. He began to consider himself, his nature and his actions, of which no one else could be aware. Yet if some friend – he thought how he could devote himself to this friend. But there was no one. He turned to his word list.

aequor	*aequoris*	*sea*
ebur	*eboris*	*ivory*
soror	*sororis*	*sister*
soror	*sororis*	*sister*
soror	*sororis*	*sister*

Beneath the repetition of this chaste Latin rhythm there seemed the beautiful words of a Roman boy to his sister. He isolated the word 'soror' which had a different tone from the English 'sister'. He wished bitterly that he was a boy in ancient Rome. On a piece of paper he wrote 'soror' carefully, and was charmed as by the signature of a lover. He wanted simply to keep it with him as he had carried the last letters from Kit. But of course he could not do that because it would be a ridiculous thing to do. He would be mad if he carried about the word *soror* written on a bit of paper. Yet that was what he wanted to do. He decided to write a poem in Latin, grave and beautiful, or a play about a Roman boy and girl. Surely that was what he wanted. It would be called *Frater et Soror*. He wrote the title, very satisfied that he composed Latin so easily. But he could think of nothing to say and perhaps after all it was rather silly. Pausing uncertainly, he remembered that he had kept the letters which Kit had written to him, pasted in an old stamp album. He decided to entitle the book of letters *Epistolae Meae Sororis*, and later he would make a Latin inscription. When they heard the bell for tea, Randal closed his books and walked from the classroom with the composure of someone who had made an important decision. He felt interesting.

In this mood he closed the door of the Green Room, crossing towards the firelight, where the carpet was ruffled grey under the dead electric light. There was no one in the room and he sat in his corner of the sofa. The fire showed the long green curtains, staring in his eyes like someone sitting opposite. He sat quietly, wishing that they would come, or that he was someone different and could be talking now to – Scott perhaps, the prefect whom they called Jock. The door opened and they began to come in.

'Leave the light,' he said. 'It's all right as it is.'

Bourne foresaw a ghost story, sitting down beside Randal.

'There won't be many here,' he said. 'Hadfield's got a conker tournament. They're all in the Big School.'

'Stupid,' Randal said.

Hayley's head, like an O-Cedar mop, and Toone's peered round the door, and they rushed to the fire.

'Just right for toast,' said Hayley.

'And all to ourselves.'

Hilton came in with a book about ships under his arm, drifted his hand to the light switch, said, 'Oh, hullo', dropped his hand and came towards them. Bayliss hurriedly shut the door, announcing, 'No one else'll be here', and pleased with himself, settled down on the hearthrug. Randal stirred restlessly on the sofa.

'Shall we play the Truth Game?' Bourne said.

Randal's heart leapt as if he were faced by a danger which unconsciously he had for long courted. Hayley quickly inspected his toast and Hilton slipped his book down the arm of his chair. They began. The foolish questions went back and forth as the minutes passed. One had failed to clean his teeth, another rarely wrote home, Mole for one was the most hated, and twice someone had voted Felton the most hated and the most feared boy. An impatience of which he was strangely afraid began to possess Randal. As the last bell approached through the inconclusive questions and answers his turn came again and he carefully asked Bourne whom he thought the most conceited in the school. Bourne quickly answered 'Colshaw'.

'You think so?' Randal said.

He watched in disappointment the black shades among Hayley and Toone, crouching over the fire. He saw Bayliss, with his still face and curly yellow hair, across which spidered the wraith of a toasting-fork like the tremble of dry grass over a face asleep in the sun. The black hollows each side of the fireplace and the darkness, so near that

Bayliss's shadow was lost in it, gave the circle round the fire the atmosphere of a gypsy camp, where the gipsies would brood over the camp fire, telling strange fortunes; and all night men would be coming from the blackness surrounding them to whisper something and disappear back into the dark. He heard Bourne speak his name.

'Who do you like best, except anyone in this room?'

Randal vaguely believed that he had always wanted this question. But he waited a long time as if he were thinking of something else or, satisfied at last, he wanted to fall asleep while Hayley and Toone went on toasting for ever. His answer disappointed him in the same way as had Bourne's.

'Scott,' he said.

The general surprise was a certain recompense. Scott after all was a friend of Colshaw. Next time, he decided, he would be really sensational. There was a quietness in the room, as the questions narrowed towards their last secrets, and as the shadows encroached on the firelight. Toone had asked Bayliss something and now Bayliss was inventing an intricate question for Randal.

'If you had to throw everyone off a tower except one, who would you save out of . . .'

He selected a random supply of names.

'Colshaw, Toone, Felton, Scott, Hilton and Harding – and Bourne,' he added, enjoying his list.

The question awoke and agitated Randal as if Bayliss had struck him. Bayliss was smiling, anxious and pleased with himself. Randal stared into his face and said:

'Felton.'

He wanted to stop the game. He wanted to go. But Bayliss said:

'Before, you chose Scott. And he was on the list.'

From the outside world the bell clattered. Randal got up and went quickly to the door.

'Turn out the light,' he called from the passage.

'Idiot,' said Bayliss. 'It's not on.'

The summer term forced the evacuation of the Green Room. At six the sun had passed the windows so that the furniture seemed to lack dust sheets, the room needed locking until the winter. The fire was unlighted and the curtains not drawn and the sofa and armchair stayed against the wall. If there had been a fire under the iron arch and rain outside, no one except a few new boys would have collected here, since Hayley and Toone had left and most of the others had moved into higher forms. Hilton was on second game and in Form V. Things had changed and Randal felt behind him the weight of two full years whilst in the present only a habit inconsequently remained. It was impossible to stay entrenched. All his old communications were cut and together with Bourne he had to take new bearings and find new bases.

One evening, Little Willie had been talking to Randal after prep explaining at length something which had puzzled him during his history lesson. Leaving the Big School he went looking for everyone, only to find the classrooms and passages deserted. He ran through the Lobby, and crashed open the outside doors. There was no one on the terrace except Bourne, who was standing by the gate into the garden. He thought out his friends. Marsden and Hadfield had gone off on bicycles. In the Paddock Marsden kept guinea-pigs, long-haired Peru and Abyssinian ones, and his friends could go there after prep. Hilton would be there and perhaps Harding, who spent his breaks at the North End. He could think of no one else, so he went down the steps and over the gravel to the shade where Bourne stood.

They looked down over the railings where Randal could hear a game going on in the garden, and beneath their quiet appearance an angry disgust made it hard for him to be patient. 'Why must Bourne stand here? No one else would waste an evening like this – and all the things we could do!' He remembered that they might be seen together and someone would mock them. He was ashamed of Bourne. The sound of the game filled the summer air beneath them.

'I'm going down,' Randal said. 'Are you coming?'

He swung open the gate and ran down the steps into the garden, and then along the path and quickly out of sight. Bourne pulled a leaf from the chestnut which overshadowed the gate and steps, and began tearing it into thin even strips. From below he could hear nothing but the shouts of the game.

After this Randal was generally to be found in the garden when prep was over. They tolerated him for his skill in finding hiding-places, and he usually avoided the position of being first caught. When all went well and he was with someone he knew, like Marsden, he forgot his nervousness of these unusual friends, racing for life up the great slope of lawn, skidding behind the water tank or break-neck between the apple trees, swerve to the left along the path to the artichokes and be caught at last, breathless on the edge of the village road. Yet it was in order to escape this mistrust that he decided to keep a rabbit.

Marsden and he had been caught in the turn by the artichokes at the very bottom of the garden and were climbing back to the green-houses.

'The worst of your place behind those tubs is getting away if you're seen. You're almost bound to be caught on that bend.'

Randal put his hands on his knees to push himself up the path.

'Yes. It's not much good.'

Marsden glanced at him.

'What's wrong?'

'Nothing.'

'Why do you come if you don't enjoy it?'

'Do you think—' Randal began.

'Think what?'

'Do you think Bourne and I could keep a rabbit? It would mean in the Paddock of course.'

'Why not? Come to my place. Harding can get you a hutch from Felton.'

'I'd rather go somewhere else. I'd rather go right to the top of the Paddock.'

'But why? Why go miles from everyone? Come where we all are.'

'No.'

'But why?'

'I'm going to put the hutch right at the foot of the Great Elm.'

'You won't?'

'I am.'

'No one's ever had a place there before.'

Randal laughed. He was enormously relieved.

'Race!' he called.

Breathlessly they struggled up the hill. From the school the bell rocked and clattered. Randal gained the terrace first. His body thumping, his stockings prickly with sweat, he leant over the railings and carefree mocked the others as they bobbed and panted up between the steep fruit trees, till fat Howell, the prefect, looked ripe enough to drop.

So Bourne was liberated from the terrace and pulled no more leaves from the chestnut tree. The astonishment of the hutch straight under the Great Elm subsided in the familiarity of the two boys on their earth platform. Strangers no longer came and the place was Randal's, a refuge where he talked freely, and had no need to dissolve enmity in a smile. The Great Elm was like a tower where the shaded grass was untrampled, away from the hutches and huts, the busy creosoted settlements built by clumps of green gorse, spiked with amber, and the rough forests of bracken. It was, too, a splendid lookout. Here at the foot there was distant vividness like that forgotten frieze of heroes, where Randal spent his life, tending Nebuchadnezzar in his hutch or hunting him when he escaped among the wilder undergrowth higher on the hill. He clenched the velvet ears in his fist, holding the legs bunched above the silver snake which shone in the middle of his red strip of belt like an imperial order, while he stood on the levelled earth under the Great Elm and saw through the trees below the village path, the glinting new wire netting of Felton's Hentown. From its black huts a thin white flagpole wavered, taller than anyone else's.

Under this green shadow lived something beyond school; munching lettuce and staring to the sea, where time was not screwed to seconds; aware only, like the free ones in the village, of the sun deepening the hours; something still munching and staring to the sea, when Randal came to prepare his bran and enter it seemed another world. Here under the huge elm he bent over the tangle of long ears and his own nervous fingers in an ever-needed reassurance. For there was something of which Randal was in constant dread. There was no tendon of his body nor any degree of his spirit which was not mutilated by his inability to dive. After prep when he sat with the hot fur of Neb's stomach against his bare knees, his fear would seem to have no end. In his sleep he would turn over to escape from the edge of grey stone by the water. At meals his throat would clench while he was swallowing or laughing, making his voice faint while he was talking, at the sight of the empty swimming bath. This dread returned constantly to a particular day. Westy had watched some new boys pass the diving test and stood talking to them by the deep end when Harding went up to him and said, 'Thane hasn't passed yet, sir, and he's been here two years.' Randal heard this, stooping on the middle step. He heard Westy's scornful answer, 'Then he'll have to pass by the end of the term.' This shameful memory which filled him with disgust recurred each day, while it was here under the Great Elm that he sought and found relief.

One morning it was so hot that Little Willie had taken his form in the garden. During the first break, they tried to persuade Scott to ask Westy for an extra bathe. But Scott leaned against the mast and said:

'Someone else can. But I'm not going to.'

They began arguing as Felton leapt down the Lobby steps on to the road. He came towards them across the gravel. The sun was bright on his white clothes like someone at the seaside far from school.

'His conceit,' thought Randal. 'Why do they stand it?'

But they leaned back on the railings and hailed him.

'Fel! In the nick of time.'

'Get us an extra bathe.'

'Go to Westy and say—'

'Go on Fel—'

'Right!' he said. 'I'll get it.'

He walked back alone over the road. They waited, arguing about him, until he came out again and called down from the top of the Lobby steps.

'Extra bathe at eleven!'

Chattering against each other, they all yelled their delight in him, and the prospect of the bathe. Randal turned and walked slowly across the road and up the steps into the school where Felton had stayed.

The eleven o'clock bell burst out in its new bank-holiday ring. The big green doors of the Lobby swung open, pouring out the white crowd scarfed with towels like water scudding through the arms of a lock. They surged over the terrace, pretending to swallow the heat, hungry from the drab classrooms, and scattering went off down the lane. Randal heard a master by the private entrance say 'They look happy enough', and Dago, with the sun in his grim face, smiled. Randal walked down in silence beside Bourne.

The first to arrive waited in the grass outside the white weatherboarded enclosure. Randal looked at the last step of the high dive which showed over the white wall, and the slender wooden rail two feet above it against the empty blue of the sky. That was Felton's dive. He did it if the water was over the chains. No one else. Only Felton. He alone could swallow dive, swinging his arms easily out in the air, as if that once he would kill himself. Randal blinked his eyes feeling the water well inside him as in a green lock, his tongue dry against the wedge of towel. Only his forehead thin with emotion denied the pale composure of his face.

Westy with Colshaw, Felton and the rest came across the second ground. Westy unlocked and flung open the door and they poured round him into the flagged enclosure. Felton with his towel high round his neck stood beside Westy. He smiled up at him and blinked into the sun.

'Sir?' he said loudly. 'Can I dive from the rail, sir?'

Westy looked at him.

'You'd be seen through half the country.'

'It doesn't matter.'

Westy laughed and ruffled Felton's hair.

'All right. Let's see you do it, Fel. The water's high and you at least won't fall off.'

Felton chased with the others to the shelter round the bath and they began rapidly to undress. Randal pulled off his stockings. He stared at the green slur on the water but he was thinking that in a moment Felton would stand naked on the rail for half the country to see. 'It doesn't matter,' he had said. But it did matter. Every action of Felton mattered, and was wrong. No one ought ever to see him. No one. Felton ran lightly without his clothes across the flagstones. The others stood round the bath and watched him. He climbed agilely, using every limb with expert and accurate strength, until he reached the topmost step. Randal stared wide-eyed at Felton's firm and active body pale against the sky. It was so detailed that he seemed to see every line. Felton stooped and grasped the rail, raising himself lithe as an acrobat until he poised there easily for a second, facing across the bath. His fingers, small and sparely shaped, were stretched closed above him; the hair yellow and straight like the grass on sand dunes, and his eyes straight at the sky above their heads and the water; his arms taut against his head like a spliced rope. He lifted for a breathless instant on his toes. His body rippled and, falling, his arms flung apart in the swallow dive. Randal watched as if his eyes burned him. The arms swung together before the straight neat body and he fell – the sinews knit from the finger-tips down back and legs to the toes – Felton, his conceit, his popularity, his danger falling as if to death through the water beside him. Randal shuddered. Through the clamour of their applause he held the slippery sides of the steps and sank into the water. His mind was stretched tight against a confusion greater than that of the swimmers around him. Lost, he found but one solution. A sole desire excluded all thought and senses: to seize Felton, to hurl him from the rail to the stones, to tear down the rail itself and the entire structure and to end that way the problem for ever. As he walked alone from the enclosure, for the first time without having been afraid and without relief, his mind rang with the idea of Felton's end.

When Randal reached the school he lacked interest even in the second afternoon's bathe. He glanced at each face for someone with whom to talk, someone lively enough to distract him, someone who it seemed did not exist. The noise of everyone returning towels to the changing room was over. From a classroom a voice called 'I'm going!' to some companion who had already gone. A door slammed and a maid humming '*I do like to be beside the seaside*' came to sweep the corridors before lunch. Randal went out again. Mr Western crossed from the private door and went through the gate into the garden. Randal slouched over the empty road to the white vacant line of the railings. His feet kicked a stone and his shoulders swung aside at each kick as if he made a brilliant pass. The alien conceit in his shoulders enlivened him. The Paddock was the place; they would all be there. He thought of the Great Elm and of Bourne and at the same time he kicked viciously the dust from a stretch of gravel. It was so hot on the terrace that the sky looked drab like heated copper. Swinging his arms, he went along the level path at the top of the garden and through the gate into the Paddock.

The gate clicked shut behind him, and he looked down the path, white between its green sides. He appeared to be going to the village, for he scrunched forward through the stones until his shoes were powdery and his toes burning, balancing with his arms and with no thought but of the shade he had left, and the haven of the trees ahead. He felt nothing but heat and sweat. When he reached the shade of the trees among the huts he stopped. Higher, a voice called:

'Thane!'

He glanced up a line of sunlight that threaded the dark rafters of the Great Elm. Bourne called again.

'Neb's gone.'

Randal walked deeper into the shade.

'I'll come,' he called.

Amongst the tarred huts and the boys near him, Felton with his hands in his pockets, pushed himself from the flagpole, where he had been leaning to watch the glint of his new wire netting.

'Their rabbit's escaped,' he said. 'We'll get it for them.'

They began to climb steeply towards the Great Elm. Felton flicked with a switch the thistles on his way. They passed the first bright gorse patches, and Felton stood at the edge of the earth platform which was held by wedges and thin boards.

'Thane.'

It was the first time that Felton had spoken to him. He stepped on to the small platform and looked directly in Randal's face.

'I'll catch your rabbit,' he said. 'I've nothing to do till lunch.'

He went to the tree and leant against it and flicked his leg with his switch. Randal saw him under the huge tree beside the broken hutch and badly levelled earth and he wished it had all been grass. He wished that Bourne wasn't there.

'Thank you,' he said.

He watched Felton go leisurely up the hill and he wanted to destroy everything that he had made there. On a mound, he saw Neb munching at the sun. A thin wiry scabious tickled an ear. They had seen him and were making a wide circle round him. He wanted them to go. Neb always escaped but he came back. He wanted them to leave him alone. If Neb could only hear them. Surely it was time for the Lunch Bell?

Neb stopped munching in mid breath. 'He'll be killed,' thought Randal. Neb stumbled quietly towards the Great Elm. They crept after him. He went faster. They ran at him. His eyes went white, his tiny feet scurried in the dust. Felton grabbed at him. Neb flattened, then gathered himself and darted deep into the hollow trunk of the Great Elm.

They came to a standstill hot and cheated. Some shuffled the stale powdery dust at the foot of the tree. They all seemed to be waiting. Felton on his hands and knees in the dust prodded a pole in the rotted trunk, thrusting it deep towards the roots. Then he threw it down and dusted his hands.

'We must smoke it out,' he said, 'get some hay from my end hut.'

They ran scattering down the hill. Felton stood there alone and Randal turned from him, waiting for the bell. Then Felton spoke again.

'You don't mind if I smoke it out?' he said. 'It's the only way.'

'No.'

He answered quickly, thinking how different Felton was, alone there with him.

'Ask Westy then,' Felton said, 'and get some matches.'

Randal ran fast to the village path and up to the gate. At all costs he had to get back before the Lunch Bell.

They were shoving armfuls of hay into the tree and a smoky haze dulled the village path. Randal stood beside Felton giving him the hay whilst the others went for more or offered advice. He was flushed with the heat and the hay and entirely happy. Felton stood on his toes, stretching to reach a hole in the tree trunk. Randal knew nothing but the motion of his stooping and rising to give the hay into Felton's arms where it heaped against his chest through his opened shirt until he fed it into the tree. This movement with Felton amidst the heat and smoke seemed to have gone on for ever when the Lunch Bell called them in.

'It'll come out during lunch, Thane.'

Felton in these words seemed to Randal to admit the almost hours which they had spent together. Then he went down to the path to join the others.

Little Willie's history lesson for the first time was wearisome, nor did the prospect of cricket or the bathe enter Randal's mind. During the whole afternoon he thought of nothing but of getting it over. Occasionally, like a fierce catch of breath the image of that morning blazed through his mind but he quickly covered it. It was too potent a talisman which he could use when he chose, but he did not choose, breathing more easily in a watchful suspense. As he lay with his eyes closed under the trees on the third ground he heard Felton placing his men on first game. Before, Felton had been a voice at the top of the field but now he knew that voice. Strangely irritated by its abrupt and ringing sound throughout that long vacant afternoon, he made himself think that it was his concern for Neb which made him impatient for the games to end. When cricket and the bathe were over and tea finished there was prep. He tried to work at geography but as the end approached his mind held nothing but anxiety. He was afraid to go back to the Paddock.

The seven o'clock bell clanged, ending prep. While Randal delayed putting away his books Felton came to the Big School door and shouted past him down the room.

'Let's see what's happened.'

They ran across the Lobby and down the steps on to the road. Randal hung back behind them who were running hard towards the garden. He came up with them crowding along the path behind Felton who had stopped at the second gate.

'Look!' he said.

Above the long shadows and sunlight of the huts and trees, the Great Elm stood in flames.

Randal watched near Bourne at the edge of the excitement where behind them the Paddock had lowered its colours for the night, warning them to go. He thought how he might leave his hutch and trampled platform, the scramble to throw tins of water into the furnace of the roots and wander, because it was over now, on the fresh twilight grass beneath the trees which they had deserted. Yet he could not move. The frenzy of the fire intoxicated him, stinging barbarously his face as if he stared into footlights or from a cliff at the gold and arrow-sharp sea. His lips were parted to drink in the smallest flicker. The warlike wind of heat and light struck his face which was intent on the close presence of Felton. He knew solely that Felton stood nearest of all to the fire which reddened his skin and brightened his white clothes. He saw him move. He watched him bend and try the strength of the hutch with his hand which was cool and remote from the fire as the trees below them. He straightened, and flicked his leg with his switch. He glanced round, looking into Randal's face and blushed, turning to inspect the hutch again. Randal stared at his stooping back, then laughed so that Felton heard and again looked round, genuinely confused, and smiled at him in friendly complicity as if to disarm his derision. Randal turned. For no reason that he could understand, he went in uneasy triumph from the burning tree and the crowd in the Paddock back to the school.

It was after midnight when the pink glow on the dormitory ceiling wrenched and jerked, staggered to a deep red; then wrecking the night came a long crack as if a giant had ripped a tent. Randal seemed to listen with his eyes. The news had come at last. Felton had burnt down the Great Elm. He sat up and in that instant was glad that Felton had killed Neb. The pink glow returned more faintly to the ceiling, and the night over the sleeping countryside was still.

In the morning Felton was the first to go into the Paddock. Along a pale sweep of grass the Great Elm burned softly among the orange flames which flapped at it like dusters. He walked around it, moving among the split branches and stepping over the boughs like an officer in the trenches. The hutch, the boxes, the wretched platform were crushed and burnt under the tree. For a moment Felton looked at it all. He stooped and picked out of the ashes a blackened tin label with – BRAN – stamped on it and tried to polish it on his sleeve. He tossed it back into the ashes. He looked down at the Hentown, with its flagpole, its huts and its paths, built in the dewy grass. Then he went directly towards it as if there were something he must do there. He met them coming down the village path and facing them, spoke to Randal:

'I've wrecked your place, Thane. I'm sorry about your rabbit but Marsden's got an angora for sale. I'll get that. And I'll get you a new hutch.'

His voice was deliberate and light and friendly. Randal was on the steep bank above him while he spoke. He could have leapt and knocked him flat on his back. For an instant he felt only a desire to taunt and attack him, to end now when he could his lithe ascendancy.

'I don't want it,' he said, his eyes staring hostility into Felton's candid gaze. 'I can get another at the farm. So don't bother.'

His face and forehead were pale, belying his words. Felton, looking up at him with the sun in his eyes, blushed again.

'I thought you'd like an angora.'

Randal wished he was among the crowd. He wished that he had never spoken or could undo his words. He came down from the bank and stood near him.

'Felton,' he said. 'I would like it. But it costs a lot. You can't get me that.'

'Listen. We'll get the angora and I've got a hutch you can have. We can fix it near my place.'

Randal heard him as if they had been talking together for a long time. They turned away from the others. He walked beside Felton, through the morning grass, to where the once alien huts and the tall flagstaff broke the green mist of sunlight.

PART THREE

Hallowe'en

Randal's third year at school was perhaps his happiest. At twelve he seemed much older than he had been before. His refuges weakening throughout the summer, he now deserted them and in this Lent term, he proudly rid himself of his old allies. Only the new boys filled the Green Room whilst outside Colshaw, Mole and many others had left. He relied more than ever on his own emotions. Without the anchor of reality he began to enter a state of blissful and dangerous hallucination.

He had finished tea and was crossing the Lobby when Bourne called to him.

'Coming?'

Randal turned aside.

'No, I can't to-night.'

'But why?'

'I'm playing the race game. Morgan asked me.'

'Where?'

'Sixth form room.'

'But couldn't you say no?'

'I don't know. I like Morgan.'

'The sixth form room? But Felton and everyone'll be there.'

'I can't help it. I promised Morgan. I don't mind. I quite like them you know.'

'You could have said no.'

Bourne walked down the corridor to the corner of the sofa that Randal had left empty in the Green Room.

Randal now spent every evening in the sixth form room. All the boys there were older than he. The bare room with its curtainless windows open, the desks straight, the light in its plain white shade grew familiar and he came to like it, even the picture of the Iron Duke with its chalked flaming red whiskers, more than the close shadows of the Green Room. He liked the boys here, their neat clean jerseys, the slippers worn by long use, the hand slipped easily into the pocket, so different from the dirtied clothes and bulging pockets, the new shoes already spoilt of those whom he had known. Randal was tolerated and even liked by them. He would spend evenings watching, fascinated, the meticulous pen and ink drawings which Morgan, the silent 'Dormouse', performed at his corner desk by the window. He would stand by the table watching Hare's new race game, climb on to the radiator to wonder at Marshall's collection of birds' eggs or stare into a locker to investigate Wilde's foreign coins.

They usually ignored Randal who could give no practical help. But at any crucial moment: a new coin, an unknown egg, the Western Handicap where the horses were named after masters and Randal alone backed Little Willie: at any culminating point of enthusiasm or appreciation – for a reason they were never to understand – they called him and listened to him with an equivocal attention.

Randal enjoyed these evenings during which he rarely spoke to Felton. When Felton played in the race game he stood silent near him or talked earnestly to Hare or swung to ask him 'Are you winning?' and turned away before he answered. If Felton was not there, he sat on top of the desk by the big window, which gave on the darkening plain, and stared down on the Dormouse drawing his intricate curves on his matt white sheet of paper, until the bell for prayers ended the day. As the term passed, he saved only these minutes with Felton, the walk with him to the sixth form room, the brief remark, the time spent near him at some game, each smallest contact. He did not understand why this was nor did he try to alter it. He only found that almost all his thinking was about Felton and these short encounters with him.

Soon Felton became aware of these odd interruptions. He would notice Thane, until if he passed him on his way anywhere, he found it natural to call out to him or ask him to do something for him. Thane appeared different to him from the others, so he adopted Little Willie's nickname for him, and called him 'Greco'. This name seemed to fit and mark his difference. Often before rugger Felton could be heard shouting up to one of the Big School windows, 'Greco! chuck my sweater down, will you?' until they became used to each other and their relationship part of the school's life.

On one of these evenings Randal sat behind the Dormouse, and was content to watch him drawing, although he knew that Felton was playing in the race game. For he was unfolding the recollection of the previous night, as he might inspect a valued gift, quietly in this corner. They had all been waiting in the Lobby, serious and excited, for the magic lantern lecture in the Big School. Felton, now a prefect, was in charge. He came with his white collar above his faded red blazer and pushing through the crowd down the passage stretched and caught Randal's sleeve.

'Keep me a seat, Greco. I'll be last in.'

He had gone, and the bell clattered and they all rushed through the Lobby and into the Big School, darkened and huge like a marquee.

Randal sat somewhere behind the lantern, against the wall, with the empty seat next to him. The darkness was broken only by the fretted light in the back of the lantern which picked out parts of faces and clothes and by the big silver-blue screen which fully lit the faces in the first rows. Felton entered. He was all in shadow until he walked into the ray before the lantern. The ribs in his jersey showed clear white on his shoulders. His face was grotesque with its black shades but he slipped his hand through his hair so the shadow of his arm fell over them, and his hand and hair were light above his dark face. He walked past the screen and was in shadow again and went to a group of boys where the windows were hung with rugs. He talked mockingly with them. Then he began to climb over the seats, whilst on every side voices called to him to join them. He sat beside Randal where he had kept his place. The lecture began. Randal gazed at the gaudy pictures telling him a tale as vague as coloured fires in a night. He was aware solely of the presence near him not so much of a known body as of a legend. A reassurance and joy filled him in wave after renewed wave throughout the evening where the colours flickered in his eyes. When the lights went up showing the dim screen tied by ropes to the window and two desks, he knew only that he had spent that hour, alone of them all, with Felton.

Now, as he thought of that evening with wonder, he remembered Kit's letters and was curious to see them again. He left the Dormouse and went from the room and down into the box room. There was no one there. He dragged down his heavy wooden box, delving among its contents for the stamp album. He found it and fingered the worn cover and the yellow pages wrinkled with paste, mistrusting its old familiarity, confidential as when they had been on equal terms. Turning the pages despite himself, he began to read each letter, intending to stop and throw the book back but always reading to the end, until he grew surfeited like one who has a cold in the head. At last he jerked himself up, his cheeks and hands warm as if he had been asleep for hours before a fire. He felt cramped, and the room was strangely quiet. He believed it must be 'late' for it seemed a long time since he had seen or spoken to anyone. He again picked up the book, to run his thumb finally across the leaves, and read on the front page, *Epistolae Meae Sororis*. Although he was alone, he frowned with embarrassment. His face flushed angrily as he tore out the page, and screwed it hard into his fist. He flung back the book, slammed the lid and made a great deal of noise shoving the box on to the rack. He went from the empty room up the stairs into the corridor where he ran and slid towards the noise that came to him from the sixth form room. He wanted to laugh or shout in derision and relief.

These old alliances had merely changed their name. On an afternoon when the hot bath after the game had again empowered his imagination, he carefully inscribed the initials C.J.F. in the margin of his Latin word list. He wrote them slowly, conscious of the rich curves of his pen. He began reading again:

aequor	*aequoris*	*sea*
ebur	*eboris*	*ivory*

and amused and defiant, he wrote with a heavy flourish the signature *Charles John Felton*. He thickly crossed out both initials and name.

In these cold final weeks of the Lent term Randal was more confident and at the same time less protected than ever in his life.

There were days of grey sky which Westy said 'meant snow' and rugger on ground hard-set like cold glue with specks of frost against the blank air. A morning came when the school awoke to a very Christmas in the windows; ecstatic glittering white wedges of potential snowballs lay pausing as if after a triumph on each open sill. Randal saw this and cried 'Snow!' with a swift joy thrilling his spine, shrinking his face, filling the airy dormitory with hills and plains of infinite wind-threshed snow. Outside, the plain stretched shining and marked with the black dots of houses and nearer, the garden tumbled its laden trees over the drifted impassable paths. It was like the still and breathless country in a glass paperweight. Breakfast was crazy as if their porridge were heaped round with presents. Dago, searching for the biggest egg, called from the side table, 'Now, Willie, you'll have to get out those goloshes you brought back from the winter sports', and Little Willie, unwrapping his brown woollen scarf and stamping the snow off his shoes, mumbled something immensely funny about Dago needing skis to get down to the Tavistock Arms. Westy came in late, looking as if his white moustache were newly clipped.

'This is it. What do you say to an extra half, Fel? Rather learn your French verbs?'

'A half, sir? I'd rather learn them on the toboggan.'

'And write your prose on the way up?'

'It's history, sir.'

'So you know all about that?'

'Yes, sir.'

'Good. Then I can see you must have it. If it snows each year you're young but once. Lord knows when you do your work.'

Since breakfast throughout the morning they lived in their own vast world where the light in doors and windows beckoned to be possessed, where the masters mocked each other as unreally removed from them in their wit as at a play, where they moved wildly in freedom and where Miss Graves hurried to the matron's room to get warm and nobody cared. During the break they had cocoa which

Dago and Little Willie drank with them, blowing gravely into big tin mugs until they all shouted reckless with laughter. It was a perpetual day, a holiday of snow where each played his rarer carefree chosen part and ordinary selves were lost. Randal waited after lunch in the Lobby under the smothered glass dome like a snow-drift. He thumped one hand on to the other covered in thick woollen gloves. The collar of his white sweater rose round his neat face and black hair, making him indeed that cold self-conscious page from sombre Escorial which Little Willie always saw. Marshall sliding down the corridor, collided, flinging his arms round him.

'Thane, I've got a toboggan. The gardener's help – the one with a wig – he lent it me. It's faster than anything at St Moritz. Wilde and the Dormouse are coming. Let's go to Trelawney Hill. Everyone'll be there. We're bound to beat them.'

'I can't.'

'Why?'

'I promised to go with Felton.'

'You always— See you there then. I bet we race you.'

'If we go there.'

'Everyone'll be going. Wilde! Wait for me.'

He ran out, calling back 'Pity you can't come' and leapt past Wilde, down the steps into the snow. Forgetting him they ran to find the Dormouse. A voice called from the changing room.

'Wait for me, Greco. The toboggan's in the drill shed.'

Randal jumped all the steps, sprinted across the terrace and returned breathless dragging the toboggan.

They climbed for some time up the road, their hands pressed on their bare knees, making their shoes crush into the snow. Randal's head nodded silently beside Felton who tossed back his hair and looked about him. They struck off the narrow road climbing into the hill where the roots of trees thrust black as iron through the snow, and huge blue-shaded drifts, covering the bracken down the slopes, almost touched the bright boughs. The air itself seemed made of snow, noise-less and still. Their slow legs seemed to have trampled for hours the trackless hills. Randal spoke to the naked hand drawing the sledge.

'Your hand must be icy. Have one of my gloves.'

'I'm all right, Greco.'

They walked farther into the hills, crossing a summit and down a valley and over the next hill. They met no one from the school, but at times they came upon a stray village boy with a desolate home-made sledge. Felton called to him asking where there was a good track. Randal liked the remote different voices that clashed through the chill air only to stop, leaving them in a closer silence. They had been given a new direction and had been gone for more than an hour, trying their toboggan down slopes that were too uneven or slow or ended in stones where a wall had collapsed under drifts, and were following the top of a ridge. Randal felt hot under his sweater. They stopped and breathing hard looked down into a steep clough, which neither of them recognized. At the foot of its long slope, broken by a dip about half-way, was a rut of turbulent snow, the watercourse which had filled the combe. Bounding both sides on their right and damming the combe was a black beech wood.

'This should do. All right, Greco?'

'Yes.'

He looked down, where the air from below struck icily at his face as if it moved past them, then back at the empty wastes stretching on every side. The place was big and soundless. Their voices were lost in it.

'It's too far for the others,' he said.

He was alone with Felton on that wide platform where only the two tracks of their sledge marked the glittering expanse which filled their eyes. Randal wanted in all his actions to equal Felton so that he would not regret that he had brought him here instead of taking his sledge to Trelawney Hill. But Felton showed a disengaged friendliness towards him. As he bent to shorten the cords of the sledge, his quiet, even movements seemed unconscious of any time apart from Randal, of any place away from this combe and beech wood. Felton's life amid the school in which Randal believed he could never share, belonged now to another age. They seemed bound more closely by the absence of the others, and every gesture they made was for each other. Felton stood lifting the rope to him in his hand and looked down near him at the unpredictable descent into the hollow shade of the combe.

They had lost all count of their falls past the black edge of the wood, Felton grasping Randal's arms, with one hand tight on the cords, and steering in some wonderful way behind him. The wry jerk in the blood as they ricocheted across the dip, the solemnity of their entry into the shade, were now anticipated by them, infallible as forest trackers. The pause when the sledge lay dead by the frozen stream was longer. When Randal leaned across Felton to gather the cords he saw again the thick sweater which covered him. He saw the knitted wool, the pattern of close-packed ears of corn. His arm as he stretched for the ropes was heavy, for he could have touched and held the shoulders where the wool was reefed like corn.

They were slower as they dragged up the sledge, their feet trudging through the drifts of snow and leaves near the wood. The shade from the combe had spread its deepening grey over the hills and a pink glow showed where the sun had set. They reached the top of the slope where the snow was powdery under the sledge. Against the faintly cracking trees and the shrubs hung with the frosted scarfs of Old Man's Beard, Felton stood and listened, as if the freezing air tinkled whilst it narrowed its darkening snow-wrack unrecognizably round them. On that high plateau, decked with its motionless white wreaths and garlands, nothing was in sight but the snow and the long wood.

'It's begun to freeze,' Felton said. 'One last run, Greco. Then we'll turn back.'

Randal had felt no dread in the lateness gathering in these hills, farther than he had ever been from the school, nor in the speed of the sledge, for he had lodged all fear in Felton's safe confidence. But when they turned back, this day with Felton which had seemed a world, endless and without beginning, would be lost unless he could keep some part, a secret talisman, for ever.

'Jump on, Greco.'

He climbed on the sledge. Felton held him, and pushed gradually forward by his heels making purple gashes in the snow. Randal felt wholly aware of this last ride. He willed that it might never end.

'All set – we're off.'

The sledge fell towards the dusk far below. The swiftness quickened his veins, making his eyes shine like a gazelle's in danger as he glanced back at Felton whirling past the unending barrier of the wood. The threat to their day slid like a weight to the edge of his mind. He closed his eyes and felt against his head the warm firm sweater covering Felton's body. The weight which he had been forced to hold revolved and fell. He released his grip against the speed and was held by Felton entirely, alone with him, Felton, alone on the falling sledge. He seemed to fall into sleep against his body, holding him safe, flying with him as on a swan's back through a world of space. Once long ago he had slept in Kit's arms on a drive through the night. He was drawn by Felton's arm tightly back to him and with one lift of the sledge they were across the dip. He laid his head against the wool of Felton's shoulder. The cool of the valley closed over them. With the thought 'This is the end' came a longing to die there.

The sledge lay still. Randal could feel himself heavy in Felton's arms. He turned, his feet dropping from the sledge. His hand closed over Felton's fingers crooked round the cord on the boards, and he pressed his face into the thick collar of the sweater. His breath made the wool damp. He raised his head and gazed into Felton's face, beautiful and firm in the strange reflection of the snow. It was terribly close to him under the short bright hair. The snow was chill in his shoes. Time was endless where he gazed at Felton and was held by him in his arms. He need never move. The darkening and glistening snow lay round them for a still instant in the silent combe. Felton rose. He steadied Randal, pressing his hands on his shoulders, and kept him on the sledge.

'Stay there, Greco,' he said, 'I'll pull you back. It won't be long.'

He pulled Randal on the sledge along the combe. As it grew dark he became a vague figure coming into consciousness and away like an animal suddenly near and lost again on the hillside. The steep hills held back the sky and the first stars over their slow progress. Randal finally lost the figure but his eyes rimmed with tiredness followed the feet heavy with snow and the now known and half-clenched hands which were drawing the twisted ropes. All the way back to the school, moving on the sledge through the night of snow, Randal watched the hands. He watched them as a duty and a right, thinking of nothing else.

They came to the terrace. They stood together in the night and saw the massed fanfare of lights which blazed from all the windows, and heard behind it the echoing stampede down the corridors and stairs.

'We're late,' Felton said. 'You can sit by me.'

Randal felt no embarrassment as he sat by Felton at the prefects' table, seeing for the first time whilst he ate his tea the lit length of the bright and noisy hall. The natural law where he was in Felton's care was unbroken, the threat of their parting unfulfilled. He was together with Felton and facing the others. Across the table Harding recounted the excitements of Trelawney Hill as if they had been exempt from some affair in which the whole school had been involved. Felton seemed to hear these accidents against an alien impression which he shared only with Randal. They seemed like two boys who had descended from an alpine mission, keeping in their eyes and gestures the echo of a solitude which none in the populous valleys could have known. Before Felton answered them he glanced at Randal, and together they laughed.

As they went out Felton looked at him.

'Coming, Greco?' he said.

They went down the stairs and along the glaring corridors to the sixth form room. Felton switched on the lights. The empty rows of desks were open to the cold night in the windows. The room seemed to have been cleaned as if for a long time no one had been there. Felton crossed the floor and against the rules shut and bolted the windows. His hands lay on the joined frames and were reflected by the flat and shining night. The door was kicked open and they began to come in.

'Who shut the windows?'

'I did,' Felton said.

Randal heard them acclaim Felton, and he went from him to the window. In his usual corner the Dormouse had opened his sketch book and uncorked his indian ink bottle. Randal climbed on the desk behind him and watched over his shoulders the thin lines which he began to draw. Felton came and sat on the desk next to them, and the Dormouse turned to Randal.

'Have a good time?' he said.

Felton's eyes were candid as he watched the snow fall grey over the indistinguishable plain and cover the hills and road where they had been.

'We both did,' he answered for him. 'It's about the best day I've had yet. Greco's wonderful to be with. He keeps quiet and enjoys things.'

His shoulders and the hair at his neck, as he spoke, felt conscious and shy of Randal at his back. He gazed where the faint shapes of snow died into the night, and felt a strange regret. It was as if he realized for the first time and with unusual pride how alone he had been with Randal and how much Randal had enjoyed being with him.

'I like Greco,' he said.

The Dormouse dipped his nib in the rim of his ink pot.

'I wish I'd come too,' he said.

Randal heard them talking. Felton's words, his last admission, were more to him even than his presence through that day of snow. He dared no longer look at him. He breathed a new devotion. The strong arms which had held him, the trusted white-clad body which drew him heavy in the darker snow, proved if anything could a friendship and acceptance which he now knew, beyond all doubt on the newly gained earth, had not changed. He tried to question this quality like a gift turned in his hands. Could he be Felton's friend? Bourne was a friend of his and he was a friend of the Dormouse, that was true, but Felton? This perfect hero, how was he his friend? Yet casually as they might say at home 'a friend of Randal' was not enough, nor could that ever be true. Did he possess anything which he would not give him? He thought exactly of the things he owned. There was nothing. He would even give him the fountain-pen with his initials which had been Katherine's birthday present. Felton was someone more than anyone he had ever met, more than anyone he would ever know. His eyes were lost in the thickening patterns on the pane. Convinced, he ceased to think for, unable to call Felton his friend, however far he searched he could find no other name for him. The bell rang from the lighted rooms across the plain hidden under the snow.

*

Little Willie always welcomed the Summer term. When dinner in the Common Room was over, he could forget the school and its tiresome boys and its overbearing staff, and getting into his two-seater Humber would drive away into different hills. Generally two boys came with him. Each summer he would tour the beautiful country with his favourite, who after a year or two would leave. Perhaps he heard no more of him, or such parts of his life as were published in the magazine, under *News of Old Boys*, never appealed to him. There had been one who had written to him from his public school. During his third term he had been drowned in a rowing accident. He had confided in his letter how much he hated rowing and now this boy had become a recompense for all the others who had gone on living without him. He was a consoling formula for these summer terms. Because of him, Little Willie was untroubled by the others.

He had taken Randal on these evening runs during his second summer. After prep he crossed the Lobby and stood at the door of the Big School which was busy with all the boys packing up their books. At last he glimpsed Randal whose preoccupied face gave him the look of a sleep-walker as he came towards him through the noise.

'Like a run this evening, Greco?'

'Yes.'

'Bring anyone you like then. Who will it be?'

'Bourne, sir?'

'Yes, ask him. I thought we'd go farther – out by Windover Hill. Have you been there, Greco?'

'No, I'd like to.'

'Be quick, then. Find your Bourne and we'll go.'

During these long drives through the Quantock hills or as far as Exmoor, they were pleased to go with a master, Little Willie, and excited as if on a stolen adventure.

But now Randal was older. Little Willie was a friend and driving with him in this third summer was an escape from school into the real world. After prep he went into the Big School straight to the desk where Randal sat. Randal had no longer the tremulous smile of a child speaking to a stranger.

'Listen, Greco, I thought we'd go out by Windover Hill. You and

Felton can call at the farm and tell them we'll be there on Wednesday. We'll need something after our walk.'

'Can't we go to-morrow? We were thinking, it's such a good evening we might go farther.'

'You were? And where did you think?'

'Exmoor. If we went now, we'd have time for the Doone Valley. Felton's never seen it.'

'Do you know how far that is?'

'We went last year. But Felton didn't come then.'

'If Felton wants to see it, we must do as he wishes. That's evident. I say it's evident we must do as Felton wishes—'

'Yes – but it's such a marvellous evening and I thought—'

'I know. Hurry then or we'll not get to the Doone or any other valley.'

Randal had the impression that he shared a secret with Little Willie, which Felton could not understand. He was pleased, for he never thought of Felton's exclusion nor that Little Willie and he might thus be ranged against him. For he had never been so happy. His arm round Felton's shoulders, the bewildering speed holding them together, he was conscious only of the moment. Felton was still, whilst beyond him the full-fledged countryside was revolving and travelling away. They were together and everything was moving past them. If he wondered at Felton's indifference and even hostility in the day, this driving hypnotized him and he forgot. He never reached the fact that this new world which he shared with Felton did not exist for Felton, that the moments from which it was created were for him as easily dispelled as a few friendly or angry words. He never discovered that this happiness, keener perhaps than he would experience again, was derived from his own imagination.

One day Felton had seemed estranged from him. His words had held a taunt, almost a dislike of him, and Randal had found it impossible to answer. That evening he had gone for the drive alone with Little Willie. In the morning he felt aloof and almost indifferent to Felton. During the breaks he passed him without speaking or even glancing at him and Felton had gone clothed it seemed only in recollection. Randal found a relief in this as if for an instant he had returned to himself. He was climbing in the last break through the garden with Little Willie who had taken his form outside. Because it was peaceful going up between the apple trees Randal tried not to think of Felton, but his words were there like the grey rot which pierced the smooth green of the apples. He wanted to be far from here and alone for ever in another world. Little Willie tall in his ordinary clothes seemed to belong to that world so far removed from the necessities of school. Randal began telling him of the diving test, hearing still like an echo Felton's cold voice. He told him of his humiliating dread and of how, almost thirteen, he still had not passed the test. As he walked beside him he tried to describe his nightmares.

'Surely it must change?' he said.

He looked into Little Willie's face which was elderly and calm in the sun moving toward the afternoon. He knew that Little Willie liked him and he was glad that what he had said had increased that secret understanding where Felton was excluded. He told him, laughing as they reached the top of the garden, of his ruses to avoid the bathe.

'Sometimes I don't attend,' he said, 'then I'm kept in.'

Little Willie was amused and disapproved.

'I can see you at Burgos. You'd steal the candles to bribe the old hag by the cathedral for sweets. Don't try your tricks on me.'

The period before the bathe was taken by Mr Barnes, the games master. History was no longer the absorbing drama of Little Willie defending the bridge. Instead, Mr Barnes read from a red textbook, a copy of which each boy had before him. Mr Barnes flapped the black-board duster over the tall desk. A white cloud of chalk settled over his black hair and moustache, and made him screw up his face.

'History, sir!' said Bayliss, who had waited for this cue in the day's ritual. Mr Barnes coughed.

'I know. And please don't shout.'

He opened his book, turning the pages at random.

'Page 443, sir, at the bottom. I put a pencil mark.'

'Don't shout, Bayliss. I know what I'm doing.'

He found the place.

'That's right. The French Revolution. Page 443. Now then . . . We were reading last time how two men called Rousseau and Voltaire had been exciting the people, until in 1789 the French Revolution began. Reading on from the bottom of page 443 – has everyone got the place? – well then, attend . . . "The mob broke into the Bastille" – that was the big prison in Paris – "and liberated the prisoners. This marked the beginning of what is known as the French Revolution. Later in the same year a great mob of women marched to Versailles" – that was the Palace – Hilton attend – that was the Palace – "seized the King and Marie Antoinette, and with the rest of the Royal House-hold, brought them to Paris."'

Randal gazed out of the window. Marie Antoinette . . . Versailles . . . Marie Antoinette. He could see her standing by a window and behind her the long mirrors full of dull November light, each had a thread of gold through them where the candles threw up their thin spires from the gilt and marble stands. Venice – Venice was all canals and at night the gondolas lit their lamps and the grey water would be laced with gold. He had never been to Venice but he had been to France. They had no fires and tall cold windows with shutters instead of curtains. He preferred Venice. It must have been lonely for –

'"—came the September massacres when hundreds of aristocrats were done to death by the mob. In 1793 a new assembly—"'

Outside, distinct through the open window, came the dry sound of crunched gravel. Miss Graves in a washed print frock, a bundle of blue exercise books under her arm, crossed the terrace to the gate into the garden. There was a sigh and a click as it shut behind her; then the silence fell back. Miss Graves – how long ago he had scrawled in her blue exercise books. Summer was longer and hotter then and the garden was much bigger. He would paint blue seas on his maps and they were like the Mediterranean; he explored whole continents while he coloured his maps. The days were so long, like a dream, and Miss Graves would go to and fro all day long it seemed, while he painted maps and explored . . . Suppose it could be a dream. He lived with Felton on an island in a blue sea. They would lie whole days under grey olive trees and feel the drift of the world go by, like the column of soldiers he had seen from Trelawney Hill. They would go down to the seashore where there were ships and Felton talked with the fishermen and they would live for ever on the island and—

'Thane, it's you I'm asking.'

Randal stared into Mr Barnes's forefinger. He was leaning at him over the desk, his arms covered in chalk dust. Everyone was smiling. He was relieved because they couldn't have guessed his thoughts.

'What was the question, Thane?'

'I've forgotten, sir.'

Mr Barnes stared at him for a long time.

'Forgotten? Then you can spend this afternoon remembering. So don't think you're going to bathe or play cricket. I don't read for fun you know – Hilton?'

'Marie Antoinette.'

'You will be surprised to hear, Thane, that Marie Antoinette was the Queen of France at the time of the French Revolution. You can write out this while—'

Mr Barnes began writing down the sentences. A door banged and shouts swung out over the terrace.

'All right. The rest can go.'

They packed up noisily, rushing out to get their towels. The door hung open after the last boy. Mr Barnes put down his pen and handed Randal the imposition.

'Mind you do it neatly,' he said.

He went out, shutting the door. Randal stretched and yawned, then strolled pleasantly to the window. Time was his and he could do the imposition now or whenever he wished and he gazed, luxuriating in this choice, over the plain. They were going down to bathe. He watched them contentedly. Their towels made a cold light under the shade. He was amused to think how Little Willie would believe that his inattention was deliberate. Only the last dawdlers were left when he saw suddenly, beneath the window, Felton. He was looking round for someone. A huge bath towel held up his head, fair and sunlit. Randal yelled from the window.

'Felton! Wait! I'll get a towel.'

Their laughter rang in the bright space between them.

'Greco! I was looking for you.'

The door slammed behind Randal. The unread imposition flut-
tered on the desk and drifted slowly to the floor.

In the enclosure Randal stared at the leaping green and brilliant
water. They were diving on every side, flinging obliquely from the
edge, smashed from the spring-board into hard balls of flesh or falling
headlong from the airy scaffolding of the high dive. Randal watched
Felton. He was totally unconcerned with the others. He saw him hold
the rail, and his other hand quench the water from his mouth; then
he threw back his arms and dived smoothly past his feet. He swam
the crawl to the side, leapt out and ran dripping back to the dive. As
he passed, he smoothed his hair and smiled happily at Randal. He
leapt on the steps, and his strong and wet hand gripped them firmly
as he climbed.

Randal turned from him to the empty water. The sun and the
water seemed now only slightly differing elements. As if unintention-
ally and at the same time with a sense of relief and inevitability Randal
dived deep through the roaring water. He emerged. He dived again
and again joyously and without thought. Some minutes later, almost
casually and unobserved by anyone and with no difficulty, he passed
the diving test. He walked back with Felton through the renewed
heat and talked rapidly to him. Never had he more enjoyed an afternoon, filled as this had been with sun and diving. His dread was
exorcized and forgotten; and Felton was at his side.

Randal was older. Already at thirteen he was conscious of his own
body and of those around him. As he climbed the steep road with
Felton during the first weeks of the Michaelmas term he sensed the
tense air of a preparation – for what he never asked himself. Autumn
fell around them. He felt a foreboding in the keen mist and the
tarnished drifting leaves, in the damp coarse smell of their blue or
red jerseys which were dirtied from the brackish grass of the rugger
fields, in the leather of the footballs and boots as they climbed from
the game. They said little for they were too close for talk, but heard
instead and together the distinct sounds, the swung gate as a darkly
clothed woman took the path through the private garden above the
road, the shatter of a pigeon as it flew through the close branches,

the sigh and tick of the dropping sycamore leaves which they ran to catch for luck. A wide sky was reflected in the wild cold blue of pools and in their awakened eyes and brows. An excitement of creation in Felton's presence gave to Randal an exaltation in these last days of October. Their legs and shoulders swung together as they hurried to the big building ablaze with lights, where the night like a huge dark sea marooned them, until they lay each in his separate bed across the diagonal length of the hushed corridor where a single fan-shaped gas jet flickered. Soon it would be Hallowe'en with its decorations, its fancy-dress party, its dances, its anonymous presents. The thought of that night throbbed through all the school's activities like a pulse. It was to be for Randal a night of hallucination, a night which after the years of preparation made the pattern of his life.

Mrs Graham's sweet shop in the village where they bought their presents had for days been in bounds. Randal went with Bourne. His face, whose bones had begun to shape their brief and definite mark, watched with another's pride, which he had made his own, the cars and shops and people of the village street. The shop smelt of cloth, liquorice and painted iron. It was so small that old Mrs Graham could hardly turn from her varnished drawers with their crystal knobs, her shelves full of underclothes tied in bundles and plump skeins of brown and grey wool and cards of pearl buttons, to the worn counter which held the trays, selected yearly for this purpose and marked in flowery lettering from 1d. to 6d. Mrs Graham, whose movements were cramped with rheumatism and who grew odd grey hairs from her chin and upper lip, avidly scrutinized the boys who came to buy in her shop which smelt to them, even on these permitted days, forbidden. It was warm and airless after the winds outside.

The trays, which they scarcely dared to touch, glittered their colours through the semi-darkness. They held everything to woo them. Their variety dazzled with penny whistles and painted wooden rattles, sparklers and paper streamers you blew with a coloured feather on the end, tinsel stars and balloons, a useless stick with a head of variegated ribbons, Chinese boxes and linked rings and masks and the gay cup-and-ball and chalks and mint rock and fireworks and games and pink or white sugar pigs, conjuring tricks and Meccano sets and flashlights and mazes with silver pellets under glass, and the mouth-organs and xylophones. Bourne stared, trying to decide, from the tray in front of him to the others. There were even a few cricket balls and a small brass-bound telescope. At last he picked up a wooden man who climbed a ladder when you pressed the shafts. He held it where Miss Graham's fidgeting ringed fingers and bangled wrists clinked the objects under his round face. He paid her sixpence. Randal still leant at the door, his shoulders loose against the post like Felton and his hands in his pockets. He half looked at the street and half watched Bourne who turned to him while Mrs Graham wrapped his present.

'You don't get anything,' Bourne said.

'I will.'

'They'll all be gone.'

Randal flushed. He saw the partly emptied trays and made a decision. He would give one present only. He need not buy it since he had owned and treasured it for years. It was the fountain-pen which had been Kit's birthday present to him. The fact that it would be recognized as from him merely gave the gift its special daring and value. The decision made him glad as if he must win by it something of great importance. They crossed the street to where the tall fluted white column of the war memorial, crowned with a golden phoenix feeding its young on its own flesh, rose before the grass of the Paddock and the line of hills swaying across the sky. Randal laughed triumphantly.

'I've got all my presents,' he said.

Bourne followed him one evening to the Linen Room where Randal wanted to get a box for his present. It was a room they rarely visited, at the near end of the dormitory corridor. The fire leapt familiarly behind the wire fender, and the maids sewed at the long scrubbed table before the three windows which overlooked the slender goal posts rising from the rugger fields. On the shelves the white woollen clothes aired, which it seemed impossible would ever be worn. Randal used to enjoy having an excuse to visit here and to talk and laugh with the maids. There was one called Barbara with blue eyes and with hair wiry and fair as rye, who during this term had particularly noticed him. She laughed into his shining eyes until he was made conscious of his own voice, whilst the wide light of the plain touched his flushed face and forehead. His conversation with her gave him the warm and satisfying pleasure of knowing more than he thought he knew. Aware of his male clothes he felt a vaunting confidence and power over Barbara. He had come once to have his torn shirt mended and had felt her fingers pressed through the thin flannel against the muscles of his back as she sewed for him, and he had experienced an almost derisive pride and command of her such as he had never known existed. He played with Barbara a role which seemed to have new and strange possibilities.

The room was changed now because of the Hallowe'en night. Half-finished costumes were heaped on the table where the maids stitched or flung back stuffs of every colour and kind whose gorgeous mass spilled over their bare arms. The fire cracked behind its brass-rimmed fender and the electric light dazzled. The shelves were tiered with the made garments which shone with the richness of ruby velvet, crimson and purples, or glittered with golden braid. The room seemed tapestried and carpeted like an antechamber. Barbara looked at Randal. He stood at the door where her welcoming smile covered his neat assured figure like that of a youth who knew what he was about. He strode to her across the room. Barbara bent her head over her sewing near his belted waist and his bare knees with their short dark hairs. Then they looked into each other's faces and laughed to cover their childish lack of wit and chided each other for nothing. Randal enjoyed this half desirous talk before the others where the lights and colours sparkled ceremoniously, as if he took her to a ball and conversed with her as if he loved her, between the dances. Bourne watched them, then turned to search for his costume, a Buccaneer's, amongst the rest. He found it nowhere. Directly under the light a Pierrot hung its long silken arms over a stack of costumes. He stared at this when Randal turned and spoke to him.

'That's mine,' he said. 'Barbara made it.'

They looked at the Pierrot which lay, a pool of white silk on the pedestal of crushed colours, down which spilled its pale and shivering sleeves. The blue light of snow glowed in its folds where the black fluffed bobbins had tumbled aslant and gleamed. Randal was pleased that he had chosen the Pierrot which had been made for him from one of Kit's discarded dance frocks. Looking at it, he wanted to wear it at once for he felt already the new experience it would cause. He turned abruptly from Barbara and his eyes looked seriously about the room. They found what he searched. Doubled back across a chair, fell the narrow form of a Harlequin with its red, green and yellow diamonds and collarless neck. He looked intently at the lank Harlequin apart from them in the cold light of a window. Then he pointed past Barbara and Bourne, and spoke as if he forgot they were there.

'That's Felton's,' he said.

Randal did not see Barbara again until the night of Hallowe'en when he collected the Pierrot's cap. Barbara wondered where Randal and Felton were. She had made both their costumes, the Harlequin from the bunting flags which had been hung in profusion for the armistice and which she had found in a cupboard. She was glad she had made these two costumes and had taken especial care over them. She wanted to see them worn.

That afternoon everyone went, as always on Hallowe'en, for a walk on the hills. The path to the Roman Camp was level. It wound along one contour, interrupted occasionally by the iron sheep gates or skirting precipitously above the two quarries in one of which ravens were said to build. But in the main it kept a steady distance over the broken bracken spears and above the road, whose cream and white stucco houses with their deep blue slates seemed to keep pace with them, for their heels unrolled the road and roofs as they walked. Under the wide sky the plain lay always in the corner of their eyes, with its map-like fields and straight Roman roads. They passed the carpenter's house where the red flowers were blown to the earth and the many-gabled and pinnacled abbey, grey and huge amongst the dark levels of its cedars. The autumn day was freshened by erratic winds which whirled the hair back like plumes from their foreheads or drove it curtained over their eyes until they had to stoop where they strung along the high path. The points of their open shirts stung their faces. Stones spun off their feet into the bracken or were hurled by someone farther along to smash through the branches or fall far below near a baaing sheep.

Randal walked with Bourne. He had no need to talk to him and nothing to say. These sights and sounds, which he had long known, fell tenuous round him as birds about a ringing belfry. The newly made zig-zag and the heel-dug ascent of Jacob's Ladder crossed the path. Some of the first already met them, calling out like relay runners as they returned. Randal hurried, calculating their pace, and looked about. Down the tenebrous avenue at the cross-roads stood the house with the foreign sentences scrawled like a prayer-book's rubrics on its damp walls, haunted or else inhabited by a spy and the words rumoured to be luminous at night. They passed it and he saw high above them the solitary hedged cottage and fruit trees, the only one on the hills, where Jenny Lind had once lived. They reached at last the Roman Camp and turned back amongst the others. The tale of the walk unfolded in reverse whilst Randal drove his switch through the dead grasses. A dread which was shot with the surety of joy held him silent as if his very breathing had gone ahead. On the terrace he left Bourne and with the plain behind him ran up the steps. The Big School door was ajar and he glimpsed the roof of streamers and paper lanterns hung unlit over the expectant and cleared expanse of its polished floor. He shut his eyes and hurried past for he wanted to know none of it until he entered properly clad.

The evening faded at the dormitory windows. The electric lights glowed palely gold on the two rows of iron beds with their red blankets where each boy changed, a yard apart, into his costume. Their voices clashed through the air amid their vivid faces and scantily clad limbs enclosed by the bare walls and beds. Randal stood naked near the door. He sensed that instant's discontinuity when the scene is shifted in a theatre before the safety curtain rises. Some had gone to the mirrors above the row of unused wash-bowls, fixing their head-dresses and peering gravely through their own shadows. They were already harder to recognize. Under the windows a boy dressed as a Tiger leaped and pranced over the beds, the hard tawny tail thumping like a knout against the darkening panes and the black rungs.

Randal forgot them and turned to pick up the falling white silk of the Pierrot trousers. He climbed into them and tied them tight with the cord. They lapped coolly about his legs like water. He put his hands on his waist and looked down where they wholly transformed him from the soles of his feet to his hip bones and navel, above which he moved naked and still himself. He tossed back his hair and leaned, carefully not moving his legs, and lifted the tunic. He let it drop over his arms like a wind against his skin. It hung clear of his neck and, loosely without touching him, from his shoulder-blades down to his thighs, with its pointed sleeves straight and long to his finger-tips. The round collar hung over the edge of his shoulders where he stood completely still. He dipped his hands in the flour which he had borrowed and smoothed them and his face white. He stooped and, whilst the silk flowed round his body like another's presence, pulled on the white socks and black shining slippers. Most of them had dressed and moved, spangled in their parti-colours, under the warm light which had blackened the panes where the Tiger, sitting on his chair, bent to tug his heel firm. Randal regarded him for an instant then, without going to the mirrors, he went out fully clothed down the deserted corridor.

Randal stood, a Pierrot, in the door of the Linen Room. The four black bobbins marked the centre of his front where he faced the sinking fire and the empty shelves and the table where Barbara was waiting alone. An Hussar's tunic of silver filigree over blue linen, belonging to a boy who was ill, hung on a hanger from the third shelf. It was the only brightness in the room where the light fell softly through Barbara's wisps of hair and upon his dead white face. His eyes too were bright as he looked across the quiet space where Barbara sat with the Pierrot's cap in her hands at the end of the table. She looked up at him and he saw again her extremely blue eyes.

'Hullo,' she said. 'It's you.'

'Yes.'

He went toward her and felt the silk rippling on him as if he were someone else. The calm air with its sound of the fire settling was noted by him like someone who listened on a plain. He felt the light on him like sunlight where he stood in apparent solitude by the table. He waited simply to go on. Barbara took a cloth. She held his shoulder and wiped flour from his eyebrows and lips and the roots of his hair while his eyes, glowing as jet in his ivory face, flickered like an animal's from the shelter of her arms and her girl's body, toward the table and chairs. Barbara felt his narrow shoulder taut under her hand.

'You're excited,' she said.

'Yes.'

'You're like someone's taking his girl out.'

'Well, I'm not,' Randal said, 'yet. Give me the cap.'

Barbara dropped the cloth. She took the white skull-cap and opened it over her spread fingers.

'Come nearer.'

Randal moved a few inches. He was conscious of his body under the draperies which were still strange to him. They seemed transparent from where Barbara watched him. She lifted the cap, with her arms on either side of his face like an embrace, making him blush through all his limbs. She pressed and smoothed the cap on the back of his head which shifted to and fro under the pressure of her fingers till he laughed and flicked his eyes. She dropped her hands and laughed too, seeing the white crown set like a cardinal's behind his wild black hair.

'Don't move it,' she said. 'You must keep it like that.'

She began to brush back his hair aslant over the silk so that his head gave with the brush and she put her hand on the nape of his neck to steady him. Her hand held him still and close to her, with his face thoughtless and calmed under her even movements until he almost forgot her, neither wanting to stay nor yet to go. He thought how he would look when she had done, while his eyes watched steadfastly her lace collar with the gold love-knot fastening it below her throat to her black frock. He thought he had never been so close to anyone before and wondered disinterestedly how long she would keep him there. For a while he was content. Barbara saw his eyes drawn aslant by the cap which fitted him tightly, whilst she held him between her hand and the sweeping brush until she had made a wave of hair curve its black arc out of the white circle of silk. She dropped her hand with the brush on to her lap and still holding him, looked seriously at her work.

'Let no one touch it,' she said.

'No.'

He smiled and she moved her other hand from him and stared at him. Faint blue shades lay in the folds of the silk about his small figure, where the sleeves covered his hands. The four bobbins and the toe-caps of his shoes under the wavering wide trousers shone like black lustre. The collar left a wide circle around his throat. Only his red parted lips and dark eyes and eyebrows marked the pallor of his face, and over all, the pearl white cap lay beyond its slanting line, brief and clear of an ear and partly submerged in his black turgid hair. She thought him a small and perfect Pierrot. She wanted to keep him for herself, there in that empty room, alone and unchanged.

'Promise,' she said. 'No one must ever alter it.'

'I promise.'

He looked coldly down at her. He did not want anyone ever to alter it. Now that Barbara had fixed the cap and his skin was drawn bare from his eyes he felt that his face was composed like a mask. He believed that there was nothing he could not do or know or feel within the strangeness of his new clothes and personality. He moved from the table. His robes hung pure and clean before the grate where the fire had died and on to the carpet which was littered with thread and trimmings. No sound came from the building and he remembered that he had heard them hurrying down the corridor whose silence struck him for the first time loudly as a bell. He turned with his white hand on the brass rim of the fender and looked at Barbara. The windows were black behind her where she sat in her plain black frock at the table which was furrowed and scoured by years of work. She stroked the palm of her hand with the brush which she had used for him and round her the air seemed quiet and used up as if there could never be anything to say or do there. It seemed to him that Barbara must remain for ever with only her work in that bleak room. Looking at her he felt a remote pity like someone royal returning to his castle, in that he must take all his excitement with him and leave her alone. He felt sorry for her life that she must pass without him. He looked at her for a long time seriously.

'You're like Cinderella,' he said.

He made the statement logically from where he stood, composed and with the wish to be sympathetic, by the dead fire. He held the fender behind him and his eyes watched her curiously for any effect his words could have. Barbara saw his proud boy's face which had, she thought, no more use for her now that he wore the clothes she had made, and she heard, surprised by the added desire of loss, the new disdain of his cold and still childish voice. She flushed, looking directly in his face.

'You are Prince Charming then?'

'Perhaps,' he said. 'I might be.'

'I wish you were,' she said. 'Then you could take me with you.'

He smiled and she thought that his face and eyes blazed with pleasure to be with her. She longed past all reason that he were older than she and that they were together in a different place and class and time from there, until her wish, where they faced each other in that deserted room with no fire and its door and windows shut, became for her the reality. She smiled, answering, as she thought, his meaning.

'You could marry me.'

Her voice touched like a shade the pleasure which he had felt in his body and which had made him smile. He turned his face from her and saw again the shelves and the brocaded coat of the boy who could not come, and thought how late it had grown between them in that dull room. They would have begun already downstairs. He moved toward the door and his trousers trailed round his ankles and on to the dusty floor, and he stopped uncertainly and looked back at Barbara. He wanted to leave her and because she was there, found it difficult. She had seen and talked to him, and nothing he thought anxiously could remain. The door was behind him and a pulse throbbed at his temples through the hair clear of his close-fitting cap and he wanted to go and perhaps not come back. Barbara watched him as if she would keep his picture behind her eyes when he had gone.

'Good-night,' he said.

'I'll see you,' she said. 'We're coming down to watch.'

'I'll go now.'

He closed the door and stood alone in the corridor. He began to walk down the corridors and landings which were empty and only half lit, as if he haunted them in everyone's absence. The huge building of rooms and stairs was so silent that it seemed to creak at his ears. He reached the gallery high under the dome and looked down at the Lobby. The door of the Big School was shut firmly as if it were locked. Behind it he heard their crowded voices and laughter round the shatter of a piano. He thought how he might vault the iron banister and like a great bird sail on his outstretched arms, circling through the dim light, down and down under the dome where it peered like an eye up at the darkness. He could even wing through the closed door and fly over their brightly lit excitement and upturned faces, and astonish them all. He laughed and shrugged his shoulders, then turned down the arched corridor. He assumed again his new identity where nothing could touch him but the images invented in his mind.

As he descended the stairs of the Lobby, which were grey with dirt under his gleaming slippers, he heard the clamour more loudly. His isolation struck him like a blow. He realized that he was late and alone. Shut from him by that door he knew, as he had known all the time, was Felton in his dress of Harlequin. He put his arm against the broad door and shoved it open.

A world dazzled him: an arc of gold shouts and lights and heat which swung in his face like a fist of gilded mail. It shattered on him its glittering facets, a kaleidoscope of the real and unreal and of all his senses, which halted him and dried his mouth with wonder, whilst piano notes like coins hurtled and struck glinting amidst the ricocheting patterns of its gorgeous and living colours. He held the edge of the door and leaned back. Like the drugged breath of the Indies a single and yet peopled sensation intoxicated him and he gazed without surfeit as if he dreamed. Many lanterns floated like green, red, and gold fruit ripe amongst the canopied paper foliage. Walls of silver shimmering evergreen held it aloft or flung high arches over the limitless splendour of where once were windows. It was the land of Cockaigne he watched, where spellbound he seemed to possess Aladdin's time and power. Night-dark tubs of russet and red apples were fired by reflections, whilst solitary apples hung waiting on their strings. Far at the end were the dark and leafy arbours. He stared intently. Chords and melodies crashed rippling from a bank of vivid blooms beneath Japanese palms trembling their delicate scissored fringes to the torrent's impact. He turned his eyes as if in mountains. Against screens of yew, long tables were heaped with parcels like quarried nuggets at the foot of fir-covered ranges. It was a land to dally in. Its potentialities broke and co-ordinated in his mind which saw the crowd moving over the polished floor, as no more real than the shadows licking everywhere from flames in the huge white marble fireplace, built centrally and facing the windows.

He turned and shut the door. Nearer him, in front of a purple-curtained window was Bayliss. He was clothed in a tight rugger jersey, spotted brown as a Faun. His head was surrounded by stars like night. His curled fair hair was spun into two horns and his eyes painted long and oblique like shadows. The light fell ruddy on his face and bared neck and glinted behind him in the crisp stars. His evenly shaped body, lithe under its mottling, panted like a faun itself and his brief face was flecked with shade under the slightly turning lantern. Randal saw him as if for the first time and, amazed at his beauty, for an instant could not move his eyes. Then he turned his gaze, deliberate and perplexed, to the fireplace.

As he had known the second that he entered, Westy talked in his dark blue suit to Felton who leaned on his elbow against the high carved marble mantelpiece. The fire, crackling in its brass and iron basket, threw a clean light on their legs. Felton talked rapidly and was laughing. Randal jealously watched him. He contrasted this sight to that from which he had turned, as he might study two solutions to a mathematical problem which was itself beyond his knowledge, staring mindlessly as if eyes alone could solve it. He forgot the cause of his concentration, becoming through his desire to prove this the sole solution, conscious wholly of Felton, whom he saw with a bewildering determination. He seemed to memorize him lest he should totally escape who before was never absent, or must at least learn the origin of an unforetold doubt.

Felton stood against the gold flames and the hollow chiselled white arch of marble. His slim body was pressed into the skin-tight diamonds of red and green and yellow which, without a wrinkle, barely hid his loins. His legs were crossed where the silver buckles of his black shoes flickered below his white ankles; and a black belt with a silver buckle closed gleaming round his narrow waist. An arm dropped at his side a stick whose coloured ribbons lay like servile fingers lightly on his feet, while the other arm, flexed on the mantelshelf level with his head, let fall a hand whose lines and nails shone distinctly in the fire-light. He did not move although his breathing broadened on his chest the diamonds, which cut a circle to free his collar-bones and neck to the warm air and the voices. Where he looked at Westy, a black domino mask hid his eyes and nose. Tied behind the ears, it made his ruffled flaxen hair and his mouth and chin gold as if sunlit. As he talked, his lips met and parted in curves, pausing on his wet white teeth, and the tendons moved in his throat.

Randal shivered as if someone trod his grave. As the chords struck for the parade, his eyes mirrored a state of triumph, sensual and exciting, until the blood dawned through the crude powder. A strange face turned and spoke to him.

'You look fine.'

'Yes.'

The hot laughing face of Marshall, dressed as a Miller, awoke him to the other people under their varied costumes.

Against the palms Bourne in his Buccaneer's dress waited. Randal joined him as the parade began, moving slowly under the foliage where the lanterns shot their gold. An Executioner in black, with mask and axe, talked to a small Gypsy Girl. Britannia walked with sequined Mephistopheles. There was a Burglar and Marco Polo and the Bearded Lady with Tarzan, and Captain Webb in a striped swimming suit and a Mandarin and a Cave Man and a Knight Templar moving past the spangled windows. Hare was almost unrecognizably blackened and bejewelled as the Queen of Sheba, and Wilde, a Wounded Soldier in blue with his arm in a white sling, had for partner a black and red Jack-in-the-Box. He saw the Dormouse dressed as the Carpenter in a square cardboard hat and sackcloth hung with geometry instruments, and with him was Marsden with the shaggy head of the Walrus. He studied them all while they moved round. A Red Indian had feathers to his ankles; Harding was a Dirt Track Rider;

there was the Ace of Spades, a fearful Nightmare, the Scarlet Pimpernel, and two Firemen and a Christmas tree covered with tinselled snow and gold and silver baubles. He waited with an impassive face for a certain few to pass the judges: an Airman, a splendid silvered Acrobat and Hilton in curved moustaches and spiked helmet as the Kaiser. Then, at each round, he saw Felton. His hand trailed at his swinging legs the stick with the coloured ribbons. Their movement carried him out of sight. He was happy for that to continue, as if Felton and he were involved in an everlasting voyage. The music stopped. Miss Graves, as one of the Cries of London, turned from the piano and smiled in the tuneless and glittering air. They broke apart and mingled over the crowded floor.

Randal strayed amongst them. The prizes had been given out, and they bobbed for apples or bit them from the strings or ate buns, held behind their shoulders on forks, or they wandered talking or alone seeking friends through the confusing light. Most of them wore masks and their gestures were impersonal yet excited while they waited for the presents. The heat had curled the leaves of the evergreens, and some flower petals had dropped or been broken, but the light was unchanging and timeless and none thought of the chill wind outside which stripped the trees grey as it hurried toward night and the next day. They lived, as children must, permanently in the present. No one entered, and they existed for themselves amongst the rootless evergreens making the real walls forgotten, under a sky of tangled paper and hot lanterns, in a narrow space which seemed large as a city. They moved to the music, over the bronze and gold chrysanthemums, while their characters seemed formed by the very clothes they wore. No longer did the place, their costumes or actions seem strange to Randal, who wandered at home there in his flowing silk. He seemed to converse without words, as if in a dream world, with Felton. This constant duologue bemused him whilst he gazed before the starry curtain where Bayliss had stood. By the fireplace Little Willie was a Spanish Grandee. Randal watched him, then on a sure impulse turned past the piano banked in flowers and entered the small arbour beyond.

No one was there. The dim green light through the yew was steeped in the bitter chrysanthemums' scent and halted him at that sensation amongst the laurels which he had felt years ago. Never was its secret so potent, so nearly conscious, as if it were physical. He stooped and, against all the evening's rules, pulled an apple from the string across the swept floor. He felt the shift of silk and every slightest sound, so tensed was he by that pungent scent. He bit the cold apple. Before his teeth met, he glimpsed the chequered colours against the rustling dark foliage, and the limbs, the broad chest and the masked face of Harlequin. The apple stayed motionless in his hand against his parted lips, while his eyes watched steadily across it. Felton entered and smiled.

'Greco! Where on earth have you been?'

He bit the apple and swallowed.

'Nowhere,' he said.

Felton stood so close that Randal saw the ribs of the material from the corded circle round his throat, beneath the colours and down his firm legs. He could almost himself feel the hard shining belt pressed into the Harlequin's stomach. His slender breathing became part of his own, whilst he heard no other sound, for their intimacy in that green arbour filled his senses. The duologue he had seemed to share with Felton had caught his words as if in a net through which he dared not break. When he spoke it was as if he were someone else from the remote world.

'You look fine.'

Felton moved closer.

'You've got an apple?' he said.

'Have a bite.'

Randal lifted the apple so that his hand was by the arc of Felton's neck. Felton bent and dug his teeth into the apple. He tugged and stood back, eating.

'Again.'

Felton's teeth made a white gash in the less white fruit where Randal's fingers curved beneath them on the hard lacquer red. Randal was aware of the drifting silk over the fluted columns of trousers which scarcely touched his body, and this only stressed the more his closeness to Felton's almost suppliant form. He looked down on the black tape of the mask rucking the short gold hair and on the least stir of a muscle. He was as sensuously aware toward Felton in that shadowy arbour as he had been toward Barbara when he had stood within her arms in the darkening Linen Room and had blushed. Now the roles were reversed. He saw Felton tear a piece from the apple and rise.

'Again,' he said.

Felton glanced at him, then stooped obediently to bite the apple. His black mask, eyeless where his fair head bowed over Randal's hand, seemed to hold him blindfold like the communicant of a secret mass. Randal fed him. He felt him wholly in his power. He knew that emotion, which power as much as a gentler quality may give, as if possessing, he could never harm his yielded body. Felton stood apart, eating his piece from the apple and looking at him. Randal laughed. He bit deep into the faint green teeth marks. He ate as if it were a banquet, gay under the shining arc of his cap before Harlequin who stood, patient and spare, against the dark walls. Never could he be nearer anyone than for that measureless instant. A shout came from outside. Felton touched with his beribboned stick Randal's hand which held the apple they had shared.

'They're giving out the presents,' he said. 'Let's go.'

Felton swung so that his red and green and yellow diamonds flickered in the dimness as if seen through a mirror.

At the long table they threw out the presents. Randal came to the edge of the crowd. The parcels flew to their upflung hands amidst the shouted names, scarcely missing the linked streamers and lanterns. The floor was littered with tinselled string and paper. Randal pushed into the throng. He felt their sparsely clad limbs, their heated faces, and breath struggle against him, so that he laughed, shoving them from him. Flung and buffeted he caught the presents, deeper among the eel-like sweating bodies leaping, yelling, catching, laughing as if amid rapids. His back and chest in his thin garments were prisoned between their elbows and shoulders. Under the showering largess, he breathed the sensual air of their voices and competing limbs. The torn wrappings trailed to his feet like sea wrack and the presents piled red, striped and gold like precarious treasure on his arms. He broke from them towards the farthest edge of the crowd. The tables were all but bare and some already walked back down the emptied room.

Under a blurred window which gave on the corridor Randal saw the maids, and at the end by the side door overhung with creepers, was Barbara. She saw him. He breathed rapidly, his hand round the base of the presents. His upper lip was pearled with sweat. His face was blank, suffused by the turmoil which had dazzled him, and his eyes were dark and cool, turned still to the details of the arbour. He stood before Barbara, his presents heaped above his wide falling sleeves, and his enchanted eyes stared seriously into her face.

'You look as if you'd seen in a mirror,' she said.

'Mirror?'

'Hallowe'en, you see your future lover behind you in a mirror.'

Unthinking he glanced over his shoulder, and saw leaving the tables the crowd of boys strolling back across the floor.

'There isn't a mirror,' he said.

His terse bewilderment, despite himself, delighted her. She was glad to see him, the small unaltered Pierrot, who seemed to be unrest-ful, and more than ever she wanted him to be like that always near her. She drew his look back to her.

'You wouldn't need a mirror,' she said.

Her quiet promising voice seemed to entrap him so that he stepped back from her. She pored on his least detail. He could not after all have so quickly changed. She gazed, despite his lack of response, down the burnished folds of his raiment under the red lantern. His cold hand held the toys. The powder was brushed from his dark lashes and eyebrows which were more a youth's than a boy's, under the white arc which barely held his ragged hair. She spoke to prove him even yet hers through his sullen or perplexed regard.

'You let no one touch your cap,' she said.

'No.'

'Like I asked you.'

He moved impatiently. He turned from her with the assumed in-attention of one who, dissembling the reason, ignores a certain glade during a walk, and takes a different way. He went to the corridor window. He had scarcely seen her. The black frock with the gold love-knot, the rye hair and blue eyes were merely the imprint on his mind of one he had gladly seen in the Linen Room. His desire to leave her was perhaps too an echo. For he was not sure what he wanted to leave, a conversation, a person or a threat. He wished at the same time to lose the silly presents. He cascaded them on to the window ledge where several, unopened, fell to the floor.

'I'll leave these,' he said.

He spoke to the frosted panes as if he abandoned a place which compromised him. Then he turned and went down the room. Barbara followed for a moment then stopped, watching him wander past the crowd.

Everywhere they were dancing under the gold-brocaded and lit red lanterns. Streamers flew linking them like the briars of an ancient tapestry where many held ribboned wands or trumpets as they whirled amidst the music from the dying bower. Randal reached the fireplace where the ashes had spilled white on the marble hearth. He stood before the arch, his arm with its falling sleeve flexed on the high shelf, and from the calm of that stolen attitude he surveyed their merging colours and antics. A content filled his veins as if he could watch them for ever. He pushed himself from the mantelpiece, going by the verdant edge of the room. The lanterns, flickering or sunk to a dead shade of red, cast lengthy shadows or sudden blares of light as from a bonfire. The dancers swirled at his shoulder like the Prince's guests in Edgar Allan Poe's tale of *The Masque of the Red Death*, whose wild gaiety persisted in the face of time. Round them lay the emblems of decay. Apples hung half bitten from the strings, buns still fixed to their forks lay awry on the tables. The tubs held bruised apples and cores and soaked paper afloat in leaden water. He walked by the piano where the ground was petalled white from blooms which had dropped or been used for missiles, and he gazed into the vacated and mysterious arbour.

Randal stood before the strands of russet creeper covering the side door. Looking back he saw Felton, weaving amongst the disordered throng, and coming toward him. A sense of wonder and continuity filled him like a cool draught of water. He knew that night would never end. Dancing encircled the lithe Harlequin whose movement he watched, for like a story learnt by heart those gestures were a part of him as the blood in his veins. Felton came and stood near him against the falling streams of the creeper.

'Greco—'

His fingers drummed on Randal's pen which he had clipped on his belt.

'It must be from you.'

'Yes.'

Randal stepped back involuntarily, as he had from Barbara when she had mentioned the cap. He gazed coldly as a marksman down his sights at the black pen, like a beetle's carapace, sheltered by Felton's hand. It seemed a worthless offering, a betrayal of Felton. The gift was a crude intrusion like a street noise from which one turns in sleep. Ashamed he wished that he had given him nothing. As in a conjurer's flash of light he saw clearly Felton's bending head over the pale gash, which his own teeth had first made. He spoke as if the gift were forgotten, and they were yet in the arbour.

'I like your mask,' he said.

Felton's hand left his belt, and tugged the tape over his ruffled hair. His face was bared to the light, and he blinked and smiled as if, unmasked, he were bewildered. He held it to Randal.

'Try it,' he said.

His free hand guarded his eyes. Randal had turned to avoid Felton's face, and he quickly took and raised the obscuring mask. Its surface was rough to his fingers. He felt instantly protected from that bright and open face, as if he magically needed no longer to see or feel more than he chose. It seemed easy to be strong and careless with the safe mask across his eyes. The stiff canvas was warm from Felton's eyes and it was as if he held there a part of Felton. He pressed it against his eyes like the rich stereoscope of his uncle when, hidden by the thick glass and velvet padded box, like a box in a theatre, he had watched the war pictures, those slaughtered men remote as dummies, and had not thought of war or death or of anything that could affect him. It had been an entertainment for rainy days. He peered through the mask and saw Felton as if from a distance, like a puppet whose strings were lost in the reddish curtain of creeper. Felton's mask was more real to him than Felton.

'I can't see properly—'

'It cuts out the light.'

'—but I like it.'

'You can keep it,' Felton said. 'Wear it.'

Randal raised the mask, this part of Felton which unimaginably he gave him, over his head. His hand as he lowered it touched the cap. His promise to Barbara halted him, like a presentiment, and he dared not alter the cap by forcing over it Felton's mask. He held it out, hanging before his open sleeve.

'It's yours,' he said.

'Don't you want it?'

'Yes – but you must wear it.'

Felton took and quickly put on the mask. He was amused and pleased at Randal's interest in his appearance. He adjusted the mask consciously like binoculars to his eyes, aware with curious pleasure that Randal wanted it, that he wanted it because it was his and that he wanted him to keep it in order to see him wear it. He dropped his hands at his sides, lowering the ribboned stick to his feet as if he offered himself at an inspection for approval, which he believed he himself had caused, rather than the needs of Randal's mind. He looked on Randal with friendly conceit and a little concern as for something belonging to him which stood alone and empty-handed, even robbed, against the autumnal creeper. He laughed and gave him, as if Randal had demanded the gift and it were the least he could do, a promise.

'Later,' he said, 'you can have it. To-night.'

Felton heard the resurgent music and at the same time he felt the magnetic pull of Randal's heart, and he turned abruptly and despite himself to go. At the same instant he knew with a strange shock that he was bound by that very attraction and even feared lest he had perhaps diverted it. He cautiously laid his hand with a new concern on Randal's shoulder. The cool unusual silk was surprising to him who had never felt it before. He lowered his hand to Randal's arm and drew him with him into the open room. Dancers surrounded them and the linked pairs banged their sides or surged past in boisterous self-regard. They were closer together than the dancers and yet, unknown to themselves, more disunited. They walked as one, where Felton for his own purpose held Randal at his side, piloting through the wooing music and the dancing under the flickering lights and the shades, as if he had found and meant to keep his bearing. The sounds and lights and movement were apart from Randal who alone was held and led by Felton, and he knew only his grip and his swinging limbs. No more existed. No more could ever be done. The lanterns swayed their erratic light on them and on the last quickening rounds of a Viennese waltz through which Felton steered with precision to the dark line of maids, many of whom had gone, and where he saw Barbara. She watched them as they came through the dancers.

'You're together,' she said. 'Harlequin and Pierrot.'

The lilt of the *Blue Danube* lifted like reflections of water from the stone heart-shaped fountains, moving its shadows of light over her face like a peasant girl's watching two boys pass in the mountain streets of another village and another time. Their life was together and remote from her, and her voice came vainly as if to two land-owners' sons passing her and proud on their path to the castle.

'You should have got a prize—'

Her gaze fell bemused over their rich carnival clothes.

'—after all I did for you.'

The music rose round them, lifted and drifted the two of them from her, louder and swifter into halls of fluted pillars and stone cornices of cream and gold, down reflecting floors where fountains played metallically to cold pools in which swayed and drifted pale images of ladies in sparkling white net with stars in their hair beneath the frozen fountains of countless candled candelabra. Yes, danced there and swayed in the arms of tall officers with spurs and a flicker-ing red line down their bold slender legs and their straight shoulders braided with gold where their partners' fair heads dreamed and lay, floating on a blue river eddying endless under weeping willows like their own gold tresses under a summer blue sky and a reflecting lover's looks and lips. Yes, danced with him encircled there where two above all were kind and true, two hussar officers, the youngest and bravest and most handsome of all the great court, their blue eyes shining with their deeds over the pearl-enlaced hair of the belle of the ball who danced and swayed in their arms, in their arms past the vast windows damasked red and looped back with gold tassels and ropes, in their arms past the dancers' dazzled eyes and the flower-embowered music which swung swifter and louder for them, for them under the Emperor's eyes and his Empress and she, she alone in their arms, for ever and never in their arms in the love-locked, heart-lost land of Blue Danube, in their arms, in their arms, in their arms.

'You should dance,' she said.

She looked into Felton's eyes and into Randal's, which mirrored them, and her voice was far-off like the closing on a ballroom of a huge door. Felton turned in sudden light with his mask black above his lips.

'Shall we?' he said.

Randal felt the flash and colour of his turning. He stood rooted amid the music. It breathed through the embraced dancers like a rising wind.

'No,' he said.

Distinctly he heard himself speak. The cotton had frayed where the diamonds were sewn together on the ribbed contours of Felton's body. He saw his exact details, the tape in his short glinting hairs, the shadows of the mask on his mouth and of the stick on the thinner diamond of his calf, every minute mark which made his shape, height and weight so that he saw him where he stood and breathed a foot apart, under the lantern's red glow, as Felton. Randal dared not be swung in his arms amid the music and lights and dancing where he longed for them to be. The real Felton stood before him and excluded the dream. Randal gazed on him, absorbed as a child is by a single fact which is for him the whole story. Felton was too complete and actual even to be touched. The music repeated its lilting phrases and ceased. Westy's voice called over the disunited and heated throng, the last dance in which all were to join – the *Sir Roger de Coverley*.

For Randal the evening in that room was ended. The dancers and the giddy repetitive tune, rotated like the far echo of a merry-go-round about his shoulders as if it were memory and he had gone. Time was dislocated. In another and continuous evening, he saw Felton: his hand flicked a stick on a chequered leg, his mouth was lit under a black mask and his teeth bit cold into an apple, his thumb thrust in a tight shining belt where fingers tapped a sheath, his hair was splintered gold round a tape and his voice asked him to dance. That timeless state obsessed him. The images he watched ceased to belong to Felton only and became, as in an indistinguishable being, in part his own. It was himself through the mirror of Felton whom he watched. Its sweet persistence excluded all he saw. He weaved remotely, a being removed from him and yet himself, amidst the glittering and fantastic dancers. The last pair turned the end of the lines and swung together and returned, and the piano struck into *Auld Lang Syne*.

He crossed his arms and felt the hot grip of hands in his. On his left was a boy's in a leopard skin, his face and bare limbs smirched red; the Gypsy's on his right were dark with bangled wrist and ringed fingers. They swung their arms to the reiterated tune and sang, and he was conscious only of this sudden tight physical grasp on either side. His tired mind seemed fastened to these clenched hands. He clung to them and they seemed to embody another's firm clasp wherein that and every evening ended. They raised their arms and cheered and, shouting, moved toward the open door. He went amongst them, forgetting his presents, where they shoved and laughed and yelled and held out to each other their gifts. Over them the great room arched with its lights and foliage and hues blazing still in gold and heat, and it seemed to diminish without the music those oddly clad boys and robbed their glitter where they elbowed past him. He looked back and his eagerness blinded him to the bared tubs and floor. Under the lights Little Willie crossed alone to the fireplace. Randal looked into the man's eyes which were entirely conscious of him, and he turned, as if rejecting him. He passed, almost last of the crowd, into the Lobby.

The dome rose black and cold, its struts like the bleached ribs inside a boat. The galleries and rails and stairs were dim under the plain lights like a sepia print after the night's colours. High along the galleries and swarming the stairs, the boys in fancy dress passed to the top landing, their shouts echoing to the crowded floor. Their aware and strident gestures seemed to contradict their carnival clothes, as if they had been caught at a legendary midnight in that middle half-fantastic state where they changed back into themselves. On the stairs Wilde in his Wounded Soldier's blue suit yawned and his sling hung loose round his neck like a white scarf. The rails and brickwork struck coldly like a tower on every side. Randal reached the stairs. He looked straight at Bayliss's face, close to him, its mouth and pointed eyes and the horns of twisted hair. Bayliss passed, then looked back as if convinced by Randal's gaze that he had spoken, then he turned again, bowing at every step as he mounted tired to bed. Randal climbed with Bayliss past the many storeys, his hand on the cool rails, the white flow of his trousers over the gritty steps and tiled floors. He watched the painted Faun marks and heard distinctly that promise of the mask and knew that despite the urgent and intervening crowd he would see again and speak to Felton. From the top gallery he looked down on the colours shifting wearily over the red floor to the stairs. He turned across the landing and, prouder in his certainty of Felton than when he had stood at the Big School door, he entered the last corridor.

The corridor was hushed under its low ceiling where the few boys strolled and turned through the opened doors into their dormitories. A smell of resin and warm cloth filled its dim length with an air of packing and preparation rather than an end. Their voices parting from each other were quieter. Behind two passing boys Randal saw Felton. He leant in the open door-frame of his dormitory, and the gas jet was turned from the Linen Room door and spilt its yellow light full on his hair and his face, bared without its mask, above his firm, completely remembered body. He leant away from the light, and his collar-bones were distinct in the shade and his smooth shoulders curved as the palms of hands. His body made a bridge across half the shaded doorway where his legs were crossed, and his fingers dangled beside and behind him the mask. His eyes followed each who passed whilst the light shot his short hair flax and gold, where he seemed to wear the gay diamonds amongst the shadow as a right. Randal passed, and Felton did not move but his left hand calmly seized his and stopped him.

'Good-night,' he said.

Randal held Felton's hand. He stared in his face, in his bare eyes blue as Barbara's and different. As if that face betrayed his memory of it, he glanced away in disappointment or perhaps self-protection. They were almost alone in the corridor. Felton laughed. He raised his hand and thrust in one swift gesture the white cap to the back of Randal's head. He shoved from the door and stood with his legs astride and ruffled the black hair through his quick fingers. Then he lowered his hand and covered in soft blindness the eyes. Randal felt the fingertips and the ball of the thumb press his bone, and the hand closed his eyes in darkness like a benediction as if he slept in the cool palm. The tape of the mask brushed and was hung in his fingers. He remained motionless holding it. Felton's hand, warmer now, seemed to enclose and drug his brain and it was as if in a dream he circled over the dark waters of a lake and in his arms. Felton moved his hand. The black mask hung loosely against Randal's trousers, and the cap shone, pushed back almost to the nape of his neck.

Felton glanced over his shoulder, and stepped back so that his colours were dimmed in the doorway. The light flickered on the vacant wall. Randal stared as if he had awoken and was astonished to see him there. He felt guilty before him, and wanted to leave him as if he had stolen from him and meant to keep his plunder. His eyes glanced again down the emptying corridor. He spoke and his voice, unable to express the unknown demands of his heart, sounded cold.

'Good-night.'

He walked, without looking back at Felton, down the corridor to where no one stood in front of his dormitory which made a square of light at the windowless far end. Felton watched him. Then he spun, glimmering Harlequin-wise with arms spread, on his heel and leapt through the door and between the several beds and on to his own. Randal pulled off the cap and held it in one hand with the mask in the other. The corridor stretched about him where most of the doors had shut and he turned alone and lit for an instant across the bright square.

Randal dropped the cap and mask on his bed. The lights fell softly on the boys who each took off his clothes by his bed, pulled on pyjamas or stared at the ceiling with his head still on a pillow. The mirrors were blurred above the washstand beyond rapid arms and heads.

Randal sat on his bed with his back to them, where no one spoke as they hurried to get to bed before lights were out and to sleep.

He drew off his tunic and let it slip shimmering beside him into a pool on the red blanket. Beneath a bare window the boy dressed as a Tiger lay breathing as if asleep, with his hands under his head by the iron rungs and his padded feet crossed and the tail dropped to the waxed boards of the floor. Randal took the cap and mask and hung them between his knees. His naked shoulders and arms and chest leant forward where his silk trousers broadened from the waist and belled out like a sailor's over his ankles and black shoes. He tossed the cap on to the palely glowing tunic. He slowly turned the mask and touched and traced the braided edge and the small convex of the nose and the cut ovals of the blank eyes. His face looked lost and serious where he shaped it as if he made it, whilst round him the room and the boys, who were almost all in bed, ceased to exist as if he had never known them. Tired beyond thought he marvelled at the mask between his fingers and wondered how he could leave it and go to sleep so wholly was it part of himself.

The door slammed on the corridor as the last boy entered. He raised his eyes and watched him go to the washstand, and the Tiger opposite got up and yawned and started to undress. Randal stood and his brain and limbs foundered in sleep. He hung his mask on the chair and drew on his pyjamas. He got into bed. Before him the days stretched in a progress so secure that no possession was needed and whose end his perfect happiness hid; where he lay, his eyes were fixed on events beyond the room which seemed to have no walls against the night and he knew, in that time down which he sailed as on a shining and unending river, no other thought or being than Felton.

PART FOUR

An Excursion

Happiness lies in motion. It chiefly consists in giving something which we possess and having someone willing to receive. Sorrow is static, for then we find nothing in ourselves worth the giving and no one to take it. A loss widens in us like a wound; we carry a small death. For Randal, Felton was no more than a facet of his necessity to give and to be received. He became for him simply a mirror of his want. In those first empty weeks of the Lent term Randal began to make demands which Felton could not accept. Then he brooded over Felton's least action, exploring the reaches of his suffering with intense preoccupation and if his indulgence in these moods began deliberately, soon he no longer controlled them. Felton grew ashamed of Randal's reproach and secrecy which seemed to involve him before the whole school. He no longer desired anything that Randal might offer. For a time he had been amused and his vanity satisfied, but now he had little further interest and imperceptibly he drew back by allowing no sign or word to be added by either of them. Besides, he had other things to do. Randal found that nothing moved whilst the unfurling leaves, the swelling grass, the sound of running water taunted and shamed his passivity. The time for happiness, had it ever been possible, was gone. Inasmuch as he knew this Randal was no longer a child.

The days went on. Behind and near the school and the flint road, the hills gave out the throaty smell of growth, of bud and stalk and moss-choked earth, of rabbit-bitten grass and peeled stick, feeding on wind and sun, until the hands were smeared with its smell as pungent as blood. He could do nothing. In the corridors and classrooms with banging doors, the library and landing and stairs, the dormitory and the terrace, the playing-fields swept bare by the breath-like wind, the paths where he walked and the windows where he leaned, there was nowhere for him to go or be. He forgot more than he remembered. The Linen Room, because of the Hallowe'en night and of that remote time which seemed now to be legendary, was especially avoided. There was also another reason. Two weeks after the term began Barbara had left suddenly and on the same day as one of the masters. They were said to be living in a labourer's cottage at the end of the hills. It was said they had been forced to leave. They were as good as dead or at most ghosts who could be rumoured to have been seen in an outlying village and who were hurrying although there was no rain and the sun shone, or who had stopped and spoken and had been daringly heard out. They and their story were soon dropped, and particularly by Randal.

He saw Felton. They met in the corridors or washing hands or returning at times from the playing-fields. They nodded as they went to bed or as they changed classrooms or as they ran past each other during the breaks into the terrace's white or lime green light. Outwardly nothing was between them. They appeared indifferent to each other and ordinary amongst the others. Randal's calm belied his disturbance for he waited for some event, of what kind he could not tell nor with what result. The days were all the same and however hard he tried he could not imagine 'anything', as he called it, that could happen. During this time of impatience when he still saw and spoke to Felton he was aware of an absence in their every word or act or touch. Felton seemed to haunt him rather than be real, both when Randal was alone and even when he was with him. For they were still often together. The car-rides amongst the other things continued as before and Felton went with them.

Little Willie enjoyed the Spring which he thought made him younger and on most evenings he crossed the Lobby after tea to find Randal and propose a run. They covered almost every road and lane and village of the countryside. The car fell steeply down the road where Randal sat between them, and the air with its dour smell of moss and twigs rose through the tunnel of trees to lift their hair. Saying nothing they were swung round the hairpin bend into the village street. The car straightened and they drove across the plain. Then Randal saw Felton alone and knew that his ways and various activities were distinct and other than his own. He asked himself why he craved for them since he knew that he could never possess them, belonging as they did to another, and he gazed in awe at Felton who, for that instant, seemed trapped for him where the first street lights flicked their gold wires across his bold and unresponsive face. Returning amidst the star-lit night toward the hills with no word said, the lighted windows of the school again told Randal that they must part, and that the next day would be the same. How could he guess that change could happen like the weather, without his will?

The days sank to a uniform grey which foretold rain while a constant wind shrank the leaves and tore into cold fangs the rapid brook which bounded the playing-fields. Randal was on the first game. During those neutral afternoons he held his mind at bay, released from the anxious hours in the classrooms or about the school or at meals when Felton's shoulders were not, as in the car, beneath his arm. That day Felton played on the touchline. His hair was blown like chaff against the metallic sky. Randal played better than ever. He scored the first try ten minutes before half-time. At the centre of the field he felt nothing but his hot breath and his blood eager to start. The wind thrummed across the plain and above their heads as if it came through banners. He scored immediately in the second half, making this try with Felton. Passing rapidly to each other the length of the field, he took Felton's pass and dived right to cover the ball between the posts. The sweat soaked his hair on his forehead and was pressed from his panting body through the tightly knit jersey. He heard none of their cheers. His pulses drummed to a desire which came to him from Felton, remote and even unconscious of him across the greying field, to combat and to win. He played solely with that aim. When the mist had fallen, obscuring all but the players, he sped with the ball against his taut body and hurtling through both the teams, he scored at the instant of the final whistle, his third and the winning try.

He got up and his limbs shook from the effort he had made and, quitting the field, he shoved back his hair and knotted the spare jersey loosely at his neck. They crowded through the gate on to the road. He climbed more quickly than the others, stooping to press his hands on his knees. He was the first to reach the silent Lobby. He slapped the echoing walls of the corridor and turned into the airless changing-room. He bathed, luxuriating in its steaming peace, and dressed. Then he watched, as he climbed in his easy triumph the stairs from the Lobby, the last few boys stream, dishevelled and filthy, below. He leant on the banister and knew in a swift vision of delight and unconcern that soon Felton would be with him.

The sky that evening was grey, furled into scrolls of dark green and ochre, recalling to Little Willie the yearning folds of cloud and hood which, with the dark boy in a ruff, had endeared him to El Greco's *Toledo*. The lights shone from the school. Randal waited on the Lobby steps, and the wide space, prisoning wisps of rain and wind, made him shiver. His eyes caught a wild gleam from the open sky, and he looked back as Felton came. Little Willie shrewdened his eyes as he watched the fair boy and the dark standing as if on a quay under a huge lighted ship.

'Are you ready?'

Randal looked quickly down.

'There'll be rain,' he said. 'Can't we start?'

A crash of glass and a shout of anger rang through the school windows as the car moved, and it seemed recklessly to echo or complete Randal's mood of triumph. Down the lane the twigs rocked above them and the air was stabbed by the first rain. Randal looked at Felton whose arm was on the side of the car and his face turned aside to catch the wind. For an instant's release he saw Felton as he was and not as an image created by his mind which, now that he had him here after the game, had no need to delude. The car swung into the village. They drove by the shops and the doctor's brass plaque and Mrs Graham's panes which were lit and glittered with toys. The white palings, the sodden grass and the five-bar gate of the stables passed them and they rounded the corner where cattle had smirched the road. The plain stretched its dark fields, drear as a warning, under the acres of slanting rain. Little Willie's rough sleeve reached to the wheel. Within Randal's arm, Felton's bare face with his brief closed lips watched the road as if he himself drove. Randal wondered with a frown of surprise how that ordinary and bragging boy had for so long controlled him. He raised his arm from Felton's shoulders to the back of the seat. He felt freed from him. He no longer needed him and he even thought with irritation that he would have had more room in the car had Felton not come. He watched the storm over the farms and fields. The wind struck them both and he widened his eyes to let in the silver rods of rain. A gull hurtled white against a writhing copse and over a low brick parapet the stream was speared with reeds like a water-logged stricken forest. The country enthralled him and arousing his old beliefs made him forget, for the first time since he had set eyes on him, that Felton existed.

The gloom of a beech avenue engulfed them. Its unnatural light shut out the plain and the rain ceased. Randal was filled with dread. He could not part with Felton for he was compelled to need him however much he wanted to be free. He could, he had long known, be happier with the Dormouse, but he said, 'I must want to be with Felton.' He lowered his arm reluctantly over Felton's shoulders. Then he felt his presence through his arm and all his body as if he sheltered, then and always, from the rain and from all else, this boy who had come willingly beside him. He watched him intently as if he owned that proud face. He consciously forced himself to think back into Felton and his life in order to regain him. It was as if he had blasphemed. Three together they raced out of the boughs and into the plane of light. He watched Felton's face which did not move against the white and dark storm-cast country. His hand, fallen over the warmed wool of Felton's shoulder, as if he now protected for himself a possession which he dared not lose, grew cold and wet with the rain which drove on them under the hood.

The car swerved, avoiding sheep. Felton lay warm against Randal's shoulders. They swung in again. He held Felton's arm, steadying them. Little Willie changed gear, accelerated, changed down again. They skirted a ploughed field and descended smoothly toward the glimmer of middle distance before the dark legendary shelves of Exmoor. The wind grew colder as the car fell towards the moor.

Randal felt no further desire in the car where their sweaters were dry as if they had long been together in a warm room. Felton's close presence released even more powerfully the images of him in his mind. He could not think of him as he was during Hallowe'en, that dancer whose arms perhaps had encircled him, the Harlequin in whose hand he had seemed to sleep, for that time was too near his remorse and loss. The darkening combe filled his mind; a long descent, a beech wood close-packed like a black frontier; escaped death closed to a body safe over a white swiftness; relinquishing all effort beside a frozen barrier, motionless; and then a slow drawing along a rift of snow, two cords and fingers tangled in the cords drawing him in possession away from the dead hills. Felton moved through his mind like the heroes of the nursery frieze. His face was lit by the blaze of the Great Elm; he spoke to him in that light morning from the village path; he called from the road when his upturned head cast his hair sunlit on the scarf of towel; he plunged, handsome and naked and perilous, with arms out-flung, through the water at Randal's feet. There were the corridors and classrooms and the playing-fields of their meetings. Randal sat by him through that long night when the magic lantern heated their faces with the colours of a storied fire. Incredulously he said the name 'Felton' with a shock of daring or joy at the end of the Truth Game. He saw him, spare and immaculate in his white shorts and red blazer, stand by the window that first night and dispel his fear by a stranger emotion as he glanced into his eyes. The story was more wonderful than any he had read or dreamed, for Felton, the hero, was alive and within his arm. Time stood still where they lay again embraced on the sledge amongst the snow.

Randal traced the wheat ears on Felton's arm. They were climbing to the moor. The windscreen gleamed like a vacant mirror, and three raindrops from the desolate country ahead had struck the glass. Randal lowered himself so that the breath from the engine warmed their knees. The spots of rain blurred his view and the wool of Felton's sleeve was damp where his rain-wet fingers caressed the ribs. He was so happy that he was afraid, and he held Felton like a shield against the wastes of the moor. Felton's past indifference and his own puer-ile attempts to break it, which had constantly annoyed him, were gone. He was safe with him and warm and at peace. He knew only his love for Felton, which he believed to be his always, and which was the more unquestioning and vulnerable, being that of a child. Outside in the other world the rain drove in folding planes across the moor.

A sharp turn swept the rain into the car. Felton flinched across Randal to avoid it. Randal held him from falling. He held him closely in his arms, confused with that other time on the sledge. Felton broke free. He turned and his face was hard with anger.

'Can't you leave me alone?' he said. 'Get someone else to plague – I don't want you. And take your hand away. Don't touch me.'

He stopped. His eyes in his drained and callous face were blank with hatred. It was impossible to imagine that he had ever smiled or spoken differently.

'I don't like you,' he said.

Randal moved his arm between them. It ached from being stretched back. He knew that he would never touch Felton nor speak to him again. Felton was lost. He closed his eyes for a second to keep the sight of him away. His head and his stomach felt numb as if someone had hit him.

The car dropped between hedgerows, leaving the moor. Then they drove on a wider macadamized road slowly to avoid skidding and rounded the corner where cattle had smirched the road. The five-bar gates and the doctor's brass plaque were blurred in the headlights. The shop windows gleamed from their drawn blinds. They swerved round the bend, changed gear and mounted the road to the school. Randal got out behind Felton, and closed the door. He called out to Little Willie.

'Good-night, sir.'

Felton turned from the steps.

'Good-night,' he said.

The car swung round and drove down the lane. They went up the steps, and the doors clattered behind them.

They stood in the full light of the Lobby. Down the corridor, the sixth form door slammed on the shouting and a boy came toward them. It was Harding. Felton saw him and his face was gaily lit as it used to be. He flung his arm round Harding's shoulders.

'What a drive!' he cried loudly. 'Nothing but rain. No more joy-riding for me. *Joy!*' he laughed. 'I ask you.'

'You're not forced to go?'

'I'm not,' Felton said. 'Never again.'

Their arms were crossed behind them so that each had a hand on the other's shoulder. They went together down the corridor, talking and laughing.

Randal felt very tired. He wondered where to go until the last bell. There was nowhere. There was nowhere he wanted to be. He could no longer imagine being at the school. He could imagine the fire at The Grange where they were drawing the curtains for the night. He wanted to be there. Entering the sixth form room he stared through the window, fearful as if it were his first night. He dreaded looking at Felton. He could feel, after a time, the cool sheets of his bed round him. He lay on the vast plinth of a tomb. Far above was the dome gleaming under snow and around him were limitless corridors where boys walked endlessly. No one could touch or speak to him. He was inviolable, the carven figure in a shrine.

Next day Randal made an excuse not to go for the motor run, and soon rain was turning the playing-fields into mud patches, so that Little Willie spent his evenings over the Common Room fire. For a time Randal no longer approached Felton even in his thoughts. Every-thing was changed and he rarely spoke to anyone. Restless, he wandered along the corridors where the boys seldom went. Strange places, remote from the ordinary school, became familiar to him. The laundry baskets were clean under the gas jet on the big landing; during the day the dormitory corridor was deserted with its white doors; the steep board stairs were dark, and above them the narrow passage past Matron's bedroom and the Sick Room had no light. In the breaks, when Felton was busily occupied, Randal tried to be near him, yet during the evenings, when he could easily have spoken to him, he sat apart on the desk behind the Dormouse. As the weeks passed he began to make himself ludicrous before Felton. If he spoke to him he chose the time when Felton was among friends and his inane words could only bring humiliation. He seemed compelled to make Felton hate him. He gradually became oppressed by that sense of punishment when the rain, like Aunt Grace, had condemned his birthday excursion. He had no friend, now that Kit was forgotten and Felton absent, to help him. The obsession grew that others did easily what he scarcely achieved with difficulty, that the boys in the lower school knew more than he, that he was so ignorant that if discovered he would be expelled. That power of fear and shame, revealed first in the word '*yéoman*', now possessed him under his '*ignorance*'. He believed that he could succeed at nothing.

Every evening he sat near the Dormouse until his guilt formed the resolution to leave the school. He would persuade his mother during the holidays. Avoiding Felton this resolution became firmly accepted. It only remained to say good-bye. The final scene ran smoothly through his mind. Breakfast finished, he put on his coat, took his hand-bag and stood on the steps at the main entrance. It was still dark. In a few minutes the 8.5 taxis were due. Felton, who went on the 8.5, stood near him under the solitary lamp. The taxis came up the lane and he turned to Felton, shook hands with him and said 'Good-bye Felton.' They move freely, and equally. Felton said 'Good-bye Greco', or perhaps 'Good-bye Thane', and they got into the taxis which had stopped in front of them. There was no difficulty. The memory of this ordered scene was like a possession which he took from the school. His life with this conclusion was clear and alone, with no more need of Felton and with no regret.

The varied incidents of the term were concentrated in the last day. The school from the earliest morning was in a fever of commotion, things to be smashed, exchanged, given or treasured, boxes to be packed, the minutes scheduled or wasted toward the evening, when addresses were to be exchanged or words between friends in those close hours of preparation before the final prayers. Randal arranged his time carefully for he was afraid to have an hour unoccupied. There was his playbox to pack before lunch, then he would sort his books, later he would take his suit to his dormitory and return *The Crock of Gold* to Little Willie. There would be other things to do until prayers. Amid all that day's activity, the laughter and excitement, Randal moved confidently and aloof, thinking of his return home when the afternoon was before the fire, the flowered walls, the closed french windows, having tea with his family, older as he handed the plate of bread and butter to his mother, more responsible as he assured her of his leaving school. He waited only for the day to end when he could hold in his heart till the dawn his parting with Felton.

After tea he searched his locker for the things he would need at home. There were very few. None of his text-books would be wanted, nor his exercise books, nor his school pens, for there was writing paper, engraved *The Grange, Otterbourne. Telephone Otterbourne* 16, and a clean pen on the table overlooking the garden. He would take his attaché case of course, where he kept his letters and private things. Sure that there was nothing else his hand fumbled in the locker and closed over something new. He withdrew it, discovering the cardboard box which had contained the pen that he had given Felton on Hallowe'en. His first impulse was to fling it back as if he were afraid of it. Then, as he held it close in his hand, it seemed odd and strangely desirable. He kept it, he could not tell why and, flushing, he shut the locker. He was alone in the classroom where the daylight had already faded. Holding in his left hand the attaché case and in his right the thin oblong box, he walked up the stairs and to the dormitory corridor.

He turned to the Linen Room. The gas jet flickered against a closed door while, behind him, a boy took his arm and said:

'Greco, I'm going to-day. Good-bye.'

He swung round. Felton stood under the dim light in a smart grey suit and striped tie. He looked at him and smiled and shook hands with him. The hard box lay between their palms, impeding, coarse and stiff and awkward, their smooth clasp. Randal sweated, ashamed as if it were a loathsome deformity of his hand which should be lanced, and he blushed as if he were caught in disgrace. Felton looked at him easily, and their hands parted. He held only the warmed box, and Felton had gone. He leaned against the wall under the foetid breath-like smell of the gas jet and he pressed his hot and dirtied hands over his face. For an instant he could feel again, as on Hallowe'en, Felton's cool hand cover his eyes. Then the intense and physical shame returned. He shuddered in an effort to rid himself of it. His disgust seemed as palpable inside him as the box which he held. He thought 'I'm going to be sick on the floor'. This last fear sobered him.

The Linen Room was deserted. He found his trunk, which was among the others on the tables before the windows, and he packed in it his attaché case. Then he crossed to the fender and flung the box on the fire. He watched it rapidly burn with a hopeless satisfaction. He wondered about Felton. He had worn a grey suit and carried a trilby hat. Only boys living in Scotland had early leave. Inverness was where Harding lived. Felton was going to stay with Harding. 'And yet—' Randal thought. The fire had consumed the box and threw its heat against his body which could feel again the wavering silk of the Pierrot. Felton had looked at him and smiled and shaken hands with him. Randal turned from the fire. He felt an urgent need to cancel his shame. He could kill Harding and take the place which belonged to him. He passed the tables laden with the trunks and pulled open the door. He knew that he would see Felton go. He would look again at his face and his rapid hands which, as no one else, he had loved.

Randal leaned from a window of the Big School. It was almost dark. The lamp over the entrance made a hollow place between the angle of the walls. Lights from the school shone on the road and, reaching into the hills beyond the North End and amongst the trees of the Paddock, the night had begun. A taxi waited below the steps. Harding held open its door with his fur-gloved hand. The collar of his pilot cloth coat was turned up. He stamped his feet and his dark careful head glanced toward the school. Harding, like Randal, waited. At last he looked at the school and called:

'Felton.'

The stone held his voice. The name made Randal shiver as if he swallowed ice. He saw Harding's short lips, turned to the light and parted over his even teeth. He shared his anxiety. Harding watched the steps as the voice answered:

'I'm here.'

Felton came down the steps in a raincoat. Randal saw him for an instant in the glare of the lamp. His face was pale and looked older under the tilted hat. He was more handsome than Randal had ever imagined him. He had a physical desire to touch him of a kind and degree which he had never known before. Felton stretched his bare hand into Harding's gloved one and, as their hands clasped, he was pulled into the taxi. The door slammed and the taxi started down the lane. Randal followed it with his eyes. His sole wish was to return quickly to school and to clasp, as Harding had done, that strong quick hand in his. Angered with shame he vowed that nothing would prevent him. He had never wanted Felton more. His desire consumed him; already he seemed to fight to regain him. A look of brutality came into his face like that of Felton in the car and, grasping the window-ledge, he seemed once again to hold him not in love but in hate. He stared into the night as if he would destroy time until it brought him again to Felton.

PART FIVE

The Lie

Randal spent the days of the Easter holidays alone on the moor. He went without Kit. He walked through the crisp heather, climbed the rocks of High Tor or crossed Black Gully, stumbling among its wet boulders and stunted roan-trees. His hands struggled with shreds of heather, the rocks, the smooth round ash branches. His interest was avid for the grey dart in the stream or the thin tarnished circle of the kestrel. He absorbed the solitude of the crags or gloried in the water girdling the brown boulders in the gully. While on the moor he was an animal of physical exertion and success. He felt joy in his hands, in the discerning of his eyes. There was no witness; he was wholly himself. His body grew stronger and his eyes more certain as he struggled toward an unknown end. If in a moment's doubt he saw Felton he would blind himself to him through a forced scramble among rocks and heather until, his body spread-eagled from a lip of rock narrow as the rim of his shoe, he would reach his hand to an ash root and drag himself to the summit. Flung down on the rock overlooking the empty moor, his body panting and damp, his hands weak, his eyes blurred with sweat he enjoyed a triumph however arid.

When tea was over he sat, morose and exhausted from his day on the moor, in the chintz-covered armchair. Sometimes Aunt Grace and Uncle Armstrong came to tea. Aunt Grace looked at him where he sat warm and inattentive to them.

'Alice,' she said, 'that school has never suited Randal. He looks thoroughly ill, as if he could do with a month at the sea. I believed the school would do him good, but it seems he's a great deal weaker than I thought.'

Randal scarcely heard her. His mother saw him, strained and small but well built for his years, before the heaped fire. She wondered whether they should have sent him to that school. 'If you come to this window,' Mr Western had said, 'you get a good view of the playing-fields.' He stood tall and fine in his old age at the open window. She saw a line of boys in red or blue jerseys straggle, a living vein along the road, from a field with absurdly tall goalposts up to the terrace. Shouting ran above them like thunder along a river. The sky was bright and the flag was cracking in the wind. A voice called 'After you with the bath, Colshaw,' and a lively and fair boy ran past the window. Mr Western called down to him 'Who won, Felton?' – 'They did, sir' – 'Who scored?' – 'Colshaw and Harding got tries' – 'No one score on your side?' – 'No, sir' – 'Well you are a rotten lot.' He laughed. The boy with the confident voice ran after his friend, and the delight remained with her of his young body firm in the red jersey, his gay smile and his sunlit hair. The boys hurried with the noise amongst them, and turning to Mr Western in the cold classroom she decided, because of the boy called Felton, that Randal should be sent there. As she gazed at Randal, thinking of that long-passed scene, she wondered with a vague and helpless intuition whether she had been wrong and she wished, however mistakenly, that they had kept Randal at home.

Kit had returned to school four days before Randal. On his last night he was alone with his parents. Supper had been cleared. The clock on the mantelpiece chimed a quarter past eight. He would be in bed at ten. After eight hours' sleep there was breakfast and the 9.2 from Otterbourne. He shut his eyes for an instant. Two hours were left. Soon they would make up the fire. Later, Annie would bring the tray with the whisky, the soda siphon, the glass of hot milk with a spoon. His father would continue reading as she took the glass to his mother, then as she set the tray beside him he would say, 'Mind you close the door after you.' His mother would take the spoon out of the glass as the door shut and put them on the hearth. They would sip the drinks while the quarters struck until ten. The usual two hours after supper, safe and unalterable. But now two hours where every minute counted. Two last hours; and then school.

Randal opened his book. He was reading *Great Expectations* about the boyhood of Pip, about Joe and their life on the marsh. Their story was continuous over the divisions of time and place like a land which he inhabited with them remote from real life. It was, he realized with a shock, the same country here in this drawing-room as it would be against the barrenness of school. A dread darkened the pages. He held the book tightly as if to keep himself beside his parents under the shaded lights. The story was his own which he seemed to dream, and he was afraid to awake to the familiar clamour of those corridors and stairs which would hold events from which there could be no escape. He pressed himself against the flowered chintz. His strong arms, which still felt his secret exertions on the moor, held the sides of the chair while he stared at the book unread on his firm crossed thighs. The smell of peat and rock possessed his body making it recoil from the unknown future. An anxiety which he could not name made his limbs ache. Held by the passing minutes he commanded, like a sullen and obstinate adolescent, that time should stop and that he could not return.

Mrs Thane laid aside her book and raised her glass of hot milk.

'Well, Randal dear, it won't be long before you're back now. It's been such a short holiday. Who did you say your form master will be?'

'Dagan.'

'Of course.'

She smiled and took a sip of her milk.

'Still too hot. I must tell Annie she needn't boil it. I do hope you do well this term. You know we want you to try for a scholarship.'

'I—'

Randal could not speak. He felt distant from her, in another world where he was again conscious of his secretive ignorance. She began sipping the milk. Randal watched the book studiously on his knees.

'Have you packed your hand-bag for the morning?'

'Yes.'

'And you told Arnold's to post your shoes?'

'Yes.'

'Because the matron's very strict about the list being complete. I don't want her to think—'

'I did. I gave them the address.'

'Well, that's right. Now I've put some note-paper in your attaché case so be sure—'

'I will. I'll write.'

His father lowered his book, and looked up.

'For heaven's sake stop talking, Alice. Can't you see the boy wants to read? Leave him alone.'

He pulled back the covers of his book and began to read, turning impatiently to the pages ahead. Randal got up and went to the french windows.

'I've finished reading,' he said. 'I think I'll go round the garden.'

He crossed the lawn towards the plantation by the river. His father's support made him reject his annoyance with his mother without bringing him nearer her. He hated his position between them. Their division lost him his security. The Spring leaves shifted against the ashen night sky and through the trees the river showed very clear and wide. It increased his isolation. He frowned at its white gleam and then he turned and went along the bank, as if away from something which seemed to trail him. He stopped and his shoes sank into the grey mud. The water was dark under the bank and farther out the gleaming curve was blackened by the trees. He felt beside him and within him Felton's presence, where he stood still above the water. He was afraid. The school confronted him like a prison around Felton. He flinched from a dark hawthorn and he felt as great a relief as if Felton's hand had been avoided. His thoughts fled to the drawing-room. No help came to him from there. There could be no escape either there or at school. The wind ruffled the flat sheet of water and the branches above him, where he stood in awe of his own body because once it had been touched by Felton. He shivered and breathed deeply to keep away the boy who was neither here nor yet absent. He said to himself, 'It's getting cold. I'll go to the broken fence and then turn back', and he walked resolutely through the grass.

The fence pointed its three bars straight into the water where the bank had collapsed. Randal stared at the small mud-choked bay. He was frightened not only at the night but at the thought of Felton and school. He wanted to go home. There remained these last hours; he could still refuse to return. He walked back rapidly and took the short path through the shrubbery. The laurels touched his face and hands and rose suddenly by his bare knees and shoulders, but his thoughts were not with them. He emerged on the lawn. The grass stretched pale as far as the lights of the house. He stood immobile. He had come from the river and through the dry tongue-like caress of the laurels and he did not want to enter the house. He stood free and surrounded by nothing on the lawn. He heard, as unconsciously he must have heard when he left the shrubbery, someone talking, beyond the french windows, in a high monotone made thin by suffering. It was uninterrupted and without emphasis like some instrument in an empty room. The voice sounded ridiculous and embarrassed him. It fell jerkily to a fierce breathing. His father's voice shouted, and his grotesque menacing shadow was thrown against the blind. His mother's voice rose and was broken by sobs and fell to her heavy breathing. Randal heard only her painful breathing behind the cream-coloured blinds. The wind which came from the river and through the laurels stirred his hair against his forehead.

Randal listened. He stood strong in his grey flannel suit which was too small for his grown limbs, and his wrists and hands hung clear of his sleeves. His face under the loose hair was set in appalled concentration. His wide scared eyes watched the house. He waited for more to happen, the crash of a vase or the shatter of the windows. The silence everywhere rooted his feet to the ground. The quarrel of his parents was inconceivable; the fact sundered his world and neither home nor school remained. He flicked aside his eyes to prove himself alone and to admit to his taut mind his swift wild thoughts. The laurels behind him were quiet. His mind chased to the idea of a *divorce*. The Grange, his childhood rooms, the garden *To Be Sold*. Racing forward his thoughts grasped the idea of himself and Kit *destitute*. The word filled the void in his mind with an icy pride. He felt unutterably liberated. Destitute, he was rid of his parents and Felton and of his home and school. He could be where he liked. No one was near him on earth save himself.

He moved. He began to pace the lawn feeling free about his shoulders, and he drove one soiled hand into the palm of the other. Round him the night was not yet dark and he saw clearly the trees by the river. He walked towards the shrubbery, aware of the vacant expanse about him. The night which once had terrified him he welcomed, at the first impact of this event, for it hid him and gave him courage. The dawn was near when he would leave for school. He was ready for it as a mere duty. He viewed dispassionately the new form under Dago, the possible scholarship, cricket, swimming and Felton as things which little concerned him. He turned when he was close to the slippery half-shining laurel leaves. His parents' quarrel no longer touched him. A new confidence enabled him to continue, which showed precarious in his thin colourless face like that of an acrobat's or a somnambulist's. He moved across the lawn towards the house. The drawing-room was quiet as he entered and his parents read, as he had left them, beside the fire. Closing the windows his attitude was assured and he knew, perhaps even then, that it was short-lived. He thought of nothing but of being in bed and alone.

When he arrived Randal at once took his hand-bag up to the Linen Room. He deserted the boys who talked around the taxis or crowded together in the Lobby. The journey through the warm afternoon had been tedious, and he had said nothing to the others driving from the station. He was tired and he wanted to get rid of his bag and have tea. Perhaps he would meet the Dormouse then, for he came on a later train. There was no one else he wanted to see.

The Linen Room had the business-like disorder of the first day of the term. It was chill and big like a station luggage office. Trunks lined the walls, and brown paper parcels were heaped on two laundry baskets by the door. The fire had gone out behind the wire guard. The curtains were not yet up and the mist was darkening the windows. No one had thought of turning on the light, and through the dusk the room smelled of trunk leather and new paint, mingled with the gas from the corridor. The long table down the middle of the room, usually covered before tea with a white cloth and the medicine bottles, was bare, except that each boy shoved his hand-bag along its roughened surface to the end where Matron checked them. Randal waited. His hand rested on his hand-bag. He would hold it until he reached Matron. As the room grew darker others came to join them, where the solemn line of boys moved past the windows in their home suits.

Matron raised her arm, pushing back the hair from her forehead. She looked along the dim room. Randal thought she would tell someone to switch on the light.

'Hilton.'

They turned to look at Hilton. He was idly tracing, with his finger, the letters of his name painted on his trunk between the windows.

'Hilton, I will not have my orders disobeyed.'

'I'm sorry, Matron. I wasn't doing anything.'

'Then why are you sorry? It's no use lying to me. Leave the room and come back when you've learnt how to behave. No, I want to hear no more. Leave the room.'

Hilton took his bag and went slowly out of the room.

'Marsden.'

Matron began checking the contents of Marsden's hand-bag. A silence had fallen down the room. The boy whose bag was being checked answered Matron's questions with respect. Every word they spoke could be heard by the others. They appeared fearful and anxious to leave, as if this were a difficult examination. Randal heard someone who had just come in whisper to a boy behind him.

'What's wrong with Matron?'

'Don't know.'

Randal wished he had waited for the Dormouse. The room was almost dark when his turn came. The twilight seemed harsh and old when he blinked his eyes.

'Well, Thane. Did you enjoy your holidays?'

'Yes, Matron.'

'Take the things out of your bag. Are your parents well?'

'Yes, thank you.'

She bent over the table with her back to the window. Her face was oily from too much work. Her thin dark hair, streaked with grey, was very untidy.

'Is that all?'

'Yes – yes I think so, Matron.'

'It's no good thinking, child. Is it or isn't it?'

'Yes. There's nothing left in the bag.'

'Come here. Do you see this list?'

'Yes.'

'Well, read it.'

Randal began to read. He knew that something was missing, that Matron was angry and that the others waited for some event. He did not care. The bleak light from the windows, the bare room and the dull and unfriendly boys made around him an area of negation. He ceased altogether to feel. He stood before her boldly, a boy who merely awaited to be hit, with the apparent effrontery of his lack of hope. He did not finish reading the list and laid it down.

'Now show me your sponge.'

Randal looked at his things spread on the table. He looked at his flannel pyjamas amongst them, with the blue and grey stripes. His mother had folded them untidily because, that last evening, she had sewn on the top button which he never buttoned. They should have been ironed, and they lay there badly folded.

'You're keeping us waiting.'

'It isn't here, Matron.'

'Exactly. It isn't here. One would have thought, Thane, that whoever packed your bag could remember that. Every other boy returns with his proper things. Why should only you be allowed to break the rules? It isn't the incompetence that I mind but the presumption. Who packed your bag?'

Randal stared at her frankly from his dark eyes. The boys behind him shifted their feet on the boarded floor, waiting for his answer. He lied. Rather than accept the foolish and passing blame, he invented a guilt that was definite.

'My mother packed it.'

'Your mother, did she? And why not you? You're one of the older boys, aren't you? Go and write to your mother. Tell her to send it at once. Do you hear, Thane? Tell her to send it at once. Now. Go and do as I tell you.'

Randal turned from her where she stood threatening him. He went between the windows and the line of silent boys, and into the corridor. The gas jet spilled its light on his black gleaming hair, where he leaned against the white door of the dormitory. The beeswaxed floor of the corridor was deserted. He leant his head against the door. Nothing but enmity and a sense of loss and foreboding filled him. For an instant's horror he believed that he had no mother to whom he could write, that the guilt of her destruction was his own. The dark turmoil of the shrubbery and the voices of his uncle and aunt on the lawn at last recoiled on him. He was homeless. Exhausted by his resistance to that last night and his betrayal in the Linen Room, he wanted only to sleep but his eyes remained open. There was no story here to lull his fears and no one to read it. He stood still as if his very breath were gone. His back and his hands were pressed against the door of the dormitory in which Felton slept. He seemed to hold it like a raft which might carry him to other times, but it held him in the corridor. Felton remained. The collapse of his home drove him to Felton but in pain rather than relief. He wanted him more than ever before and, if he could, he would have killed him. With Felton gone there would be peace. He knew, with a hopeless certainty, that Felton alone could make him secure and, because only he could cure it, he seemed the cause of all his loss. He needed him not as a friend, for what they had shared together, but as a tyrant who owned and could guard his mind and body. He loved and hated him. He flattened his hands and pressed his arms spread-eagled against the door as if he barred Felton behind him in the dormitory. His eyes shone. He was alone and he did not move.

The school enjoyed, during the next days, the first hot weather of the term. Randal felt older and completely detached from their activities so that he regarded distantly anything that was said or done. The dread of Dago's form and the impending geography test did not touch him. His 'ignorance' still kept him apart. He believed that he had reached this attitude by a process of reason. He could not know that his calm and precise manner was dissimulation, nor that those who hide an undeclared desire or fear must be false. Randal's soul was filled with these two emotions to the exclusion of all else. To lie was natural. He avoided Felton who ate at a different table and was in a different form, and so coldly did Randal appear divided from him that he scarcely saw him when he passed. Yet it was Felton who held his power to act.

The first bathe was on the day of the geography test. He dreaded, not as before to dive, when Felton's presence that afternoon had cured him, but Felton himself. He was repelled by the idea of Felton naked and beside him amongst the plunging and impersonal bodies in the swimming bath. That fear cut like a bar through his desire to meet him. He did not consider how he would be exempt on that afternoon which followed the test; he knew only that he would not bathe. He dreamed constantly of other ways that they might meet. He would run away and 'take to the hills' and Felton, as once before, would come to him. He imagined for days that miraculous scene which, being unreal, would never happen. He knew with an obscure certainty that they must meet and he waited.

The Dormouse alone was aware of Randal's withdrawal. His intelligent brown eyes watched him. He understood his mood from his face and gestures, in the same way as he had learned the bend and resistance of those fronds and leaves, which his sensitive hand fixed in his drawings. He shared with Randal however differently the need to express order. It was this, although unacknowledged, which had made them friends. The evening was hot and the others had gone to the Paddock or into the garden when he entered the fifth form room. His even features were still under his straight mouse-coloured hair, as he stared at Randal who sat reading at his desk by the window.

'Hullo,' he said. 'Have you seen my indian ink bottle?'

'No.'

The Dormouse wandered to the window, searching as if it might be hidden between the floor boards. He climbed on to the desk behind Randal and pressed his hands on his shoulders.

'What's wrong, Thanery?'

He swayed Randal to and fro before the window.

'Is anything wrong at home? Is your mother dead or anything?'

The feeling of being swayed without effort and the soft inflexion of the voice gave Randal a warmth which overflowed his mind. He laid the weight of his body in his friend's hands and stared at the see-saw of distance. Randal had forgotten his home. The plain held under the dying sun only the moment.

'Yes,' he said, 'something at home.'

The Dormouse stopped swaying him. His hands were laid loosely on his shoulders.

'To-morrow's the test,' he said. 'Will you be in the sixth form room? I want to show you my drawings. You can tell me which you like. I want to give you one.'

As Randal lay in bed he remembered the Dormouse. He liked him and he understood his drawings and he wanted more than anything to possess one. That desire for the white card on which there curved the exact and pure black lines was more real to him than his desire for Felton. He turned, restlessly dismissing it from his mind. The course of time was dislocated, so that his meeting with the Dormouse the next evening remained intact, whilst annihilating it like a howling storm were the test and the bathe. He seemed two boys, one who was engulfed by impossible events, the other whose ordinary life continued. He dreamed throughout the night of Felton. Falling asleep he came through the morning to a gate which was at lunch time. Beyond the gate he could not pass. The possibility of running away was beyond the gate. If it had been on his side he would have used it. 'But it isn't,' he said. 'Possibility is shut out with Everything else.' He decided to kill himself in the view of Everything on the other side. Everything would try to stop him but would fail because of the gate. As he fell Everything broke down the gate and caught him dead in his arms. He carried him forward and the gate was no longer there, and the land stretched empty to the white sea and the black curve of the sand dunes.

Randal awoke. The dormitory was bleak and the boys slept distinct in their beds like enemies who seemed to guard him. 'There is no gate,' he said. He heard someone cross the road two storeys below. The inescapable horror of the next day had crept several hours nearer, and the dawn could not be far. He shut his eyes tightly and dragged himself from the fact into a feverish sleep. He glided close to Felton under water. He gripped Felton naked in his arms and he was going to kill him when they reached the lagoon. Felton struck out his legs to get them to the lagoon and Randal lay motionless within his active limbs. He prisoned Felton's cold fingers to prevent his escape and he pressed them back to force him to swim faster and faster. They plunged at last into sudden warmth. He crushed Felton to him and broke his fingers and killed him. He felt him fall away and leave him alone in the dark enveloping water. Then he awoke. His face and hands were burning. He breathed rapidly and he shivered from exhaustion. He was too drained of emotion to think of what had happened. He pulled up the bedclothes and fell at once into a peaceful sleep. When he awoke it was to the clatter of the bell.

The event of that night absorbed him during the morning. His movements were not his but those of Felton who was imprisoned in his body. His eyes were spaced wider. The set of his cheek bones, the brief curve of his mouth, the texture of his skin belonged to Felton; as he walked, he could still feel in his legs the action of Felton swimming. The subtlety of the paradox filled him with delight. He repeated Felton's turn of the head or his flick of the fingers to enjoy it further. His power to possess Felton in his least gesture entranced him. He had no more need of a future.

Randal sat at his desk, that afternoon, with his books closed in front of him. He felt no anxiety. He seemed to lie against a bar which could not break and the rest of the school fell headlong past him. In his second term Kit had sent him a picture of a matador. For weeks he had carried it with him and believed that nothing during the lesson could hurt him while he possessed the matador. He had not changed his belief. The sense of Felton would wait beyond the test, like a friend at a tryst. He marvelled how dull and unprotected must be those others who were not exempted from the life at school to spend a holiday with Felton. So absorbed was he by that pleasure that he scarcely considered that it was imaginary.

Dago was pointing his finger from his tall desk at each boy.

'Next – next – Hilton.'

His chair cracked like a whip behind his voice. He went stiffly to Hilton whose mouth was open.

'Well, Hilton? Well?'

'I – don't know sir.'

'Shut your mouth then, you little fool. I don't want your germs. Next – Wake up, Thane – next.'

He stood close to the boys, and his need to strike them was concentrated in his voice. He tightened the word 'next' between his lips, as if he lashed them with it. Randal felt stifled until he went from them back to his desk.

'Right.'

Dago sat rigid. His eyes and lips appeared dry. He spoke precisely.

'Listen to me. I shall begin again. I shall ask one word questions. If any boy fails to answer correctly, or answers in more than one word, he'll be thrashed. You've got to know it.'

Dago began with the right-hand boy in the front row. The questions were simple and each boy gave the correct answer. It was like a drill display where a slip was unthinkable. Every boy's mind switched automatically from question to answer. He collected the answers in his throat, like counting out his cards in *Beggar my Neighbour*, until his 'stop' card came and he could rest. To Randal the efficiency of the process was like the repetitions in a dream. It was so unreal that he could not think.

'Thane. The port of Edinburgh?'

Randal could not answer.

'Answer me.'

Dago swung toward him, and he faintly replied:

'I've forgotten, sir.'

'You're a liar, Thane.'

Dago got down and came close to Randal. His nearness and power seemed to crush his body to him.

'You're lying. You've not learnt it.'

His voice, which reviled Randal, was thick with emotion. Randal did not flinch. He welcomed the words which seemed to cut into his luxurious thoughts.

'Answer these questions.'

Each question was simpler than the last, and Randal did not speak. This tirade attacked the sensual pleasure which he had felt since the night. Its unreasonable violence took the guilt of his ignorance and excused it. Dago's words yelled out of control.

'You've got to be thrashed.'

Randal balanced himself with his hands among the desks. He was thinking 'Fool, don't shout,' and these rational words calmed his dread. He bent down. His fingers were neat on each knee. His shoes marked a black square in the midst of the boards which were brown and vacant in the sunlight. The fingers, the shoes and the clean boards gave him a sense of triumph. The afternoon heat fell through the windows. Randal returned to his desk. His body was cleansed and tired, his mind active and without fear. He felt experienced and proud as he watched the attentive boys, who soon would be amid the clamour of the swimming bath. He believed that he had purposely refused to answer. He thought of Felton as of someone apart. He could speak to him and listen to him, go away from him and come back to him, as sensibly as if he were any friend. He felt freed as if no more could happen. The atonement of his body had restored his confidence in Felton. He made his decision. Nothing must impair his new-found security.

The bell rang and, seizing their books, they raced down the corridor to get their towels. Randal went to his locker and took out his writing-pad. He left the classroom and walked down the corridor, past the changing-room and under the high dome of the Lobby, to the Green Room. He closed the door behind him in the quiet room. The fire was not lit. The room was filled with a green light, and between the thick curtains he saw the small private lawn, sheltered from the heat by the shrubs and trees. He sat in the corner of the sofa. He was glad to be alone in this room. The carpet covered the floor under the polished furniture and recalled to him a country house where he had stayed. It had a park with tall beech trees and a winding drive and a lake with swans. In this room he felt content and far from the school and he was aware how inappropriate were the white shirt and shorts which he had to wear. He had gained an identity. He believed that in the future he was no one but himself. He bent over the pad on his knees. His eyes were cool and rapt. He began to write a story which he had entitled *The Lake*. The pen was held firmly in his hand. He was oblivious of the time and place and he heard through his happiness only the scratch of his pen across the paper.

A noise at the door interrupted him. He looked up. Matron, who carried an armful of daffodils, came into the room. The flowers blazed on him in their gold from her grey sleeve. Matron spoke in a loud outside voice with the door open at her back.

'Thane? What on earth are you doing here? Why aren't you swimming? With the others?'

Matron was right to be out in the garden, as the others were right to be at the swimming bath. Caught and defeated, as if weary of talking, he made his only answer.

'I was given an imposition, Matron.'

He looked up at her with his frank and distant eyes.

'Mr Willie gave it to me.'

Matron put the flowers on a table. Then, without looking at him, she turned to the door.

'Come with me,' she said.

They went into the tiled corridor and up the thick carpet of the private stairs. Randal followed Matron. His hand slid along the broad polished banister. The boys were not allowed on the private stairs. He was allowed there, as a new boy would be allowed on his first arrival. The softness of the carpet which hid their footsteps, the dark and smooth banister, admitted of no resistance. They reached the masters' end of the building.

'Wait here,' Matron said to him.

He waited with his hand on the banister. He watched Matron go toward the Common Room, thinking 'She's going to talk to Little Willie.' He was careless of his danger because it was too great. Being allowed where no other boy could go, he believed that he no longer belonged to the school nor was involved in the actions which he had started. He watched Matron indifferently as she returned.

'Mr Willie denies all knowledge of the imposition. As I thought, you were lying, Thane. Mr Western of course must be told. There's nothing he hates so much in a boy as lying. He's extremely severe on boys who lie. You're to go up to the Sick Room and wait there until I come. If Mr Western can't see you to-night, then you'll have to sleep there, that's all. Perhaps I'd better come with you; clearly you're not to be trusted.'

Randal again followed Matron. They went across the landing where the laundry baskets were stacked and along the dormitory corridor. Matron climbed the dark narrow stairs where it was difficult to keep up with her round the steep corners. As they walked down the passage which led past Matron's bedroom and the Sick Room, Randal remembered that outside these thick walls of bedrooms the others were swimming or playing cricket. Matron opened the door and he followed her into the Sick Room. There were four beds in the room and a row of wash-basins. In the sunlight which crossed the foot of each bed the blankets were folded into deep squares.

'That will be your bed near the fireplace, if you have to spend the night here.'

Matron turned from him and went out, closing the door. Randal heard the short turn of the key. He moved, still holding the writing-pad, to the bed which would be his. The red blanket covered the mattress as far as a clean pillow. He lay down with the writing-pad beside him. His fingers touched the rough blanket and, as if to try its pain, he pressed against it his hands and bare knees and face until they burned. The bleak sound of the key filled him with desolation. He was cut off alone, and forgotten. His confidence was gone and every sinew of his body seemed destroyed. He was rejected and wrong. He held himself tense against the warm pace of the minutes through the afternoon and the room, and he breathed the used air which smelled ashen between the shut window and the locked door. The empty silence throbbed at his ears. Then he relaxed his limbs and laid his head in the cool pillow. He turned half on his stomach, with his hands flat at each side of his head near the iron rails. He felt his hair spread as if on a stream over the pillow. His legs were curved easily and loosely toward him. He stared at the sunlight on his black shoes and thought of nothing.

The bell awoke Randal in the Sick Room. It cancelled in one sound the nightmare where he had feverishly struggled through the night, to reach what solution? The school bell meant that the identical facts were still there. As he heard its reiterated clatter he seemed exhausted and he felt for the first time with shame the pain of Dago's beating.

He began to believe that he endured this fruitless struggle every night and that the bell awoke him each day to facts which were the result of his lie and could not be faced. He indulged his exhaustion until he forgot or excused everything under the cover of sleeplessness, and he sought in illness the nearest shelter from the actual. The bell had stopped and he enlarged this idea until it became a disease. He had *insomnia*. When they knew that, it would protect him from all they could do to him. Insomnia was vaguely connected with The Grange and would mean perhaps his reprieve from school.

He took off his pyjamas on the edge of the bed. As he flung them aside he flinched and exaggerated his shudder from the cold. The muscles of his back and arms were hard as he pulled on his shirt and fastened the belt round his shorts, and his fingers were well formed and supple, winding tightly the knitted garters round his stockings, which he neatly reversed to meet the tasselled fringes. He stared at his hands on his firm legs and saw his strong knees with the short dark hairs. His body felt active, like some young animal trapped and immobile, and he frowned, straining his forehead, to keep in it its disease. He dared not be himself and strong. He needed the disease as he needed the lie which it would cover. It was as if he had chosen to lie, so completely had it concealed his thoughts and absolved him from all other action. It was more important than anything he could now do and its consequences alone occupied his mind. He moved carefully and already dressed about the room. The magnitude of the lie and his inability to alter it gave him a sense of release. He turned down his bedclothes and went calmly into the deserted passage.

During the morning, in the breaks and throughout each lesson, he felt the boys loathing his liar's face. Something, he knew, must happen. He dreaded the summons to Westy's study. He wondered constantly how he could report his insomnia in time to prevent them sending for him. Every anguish of suspense was enacted through his body: the ache which groped behind his eyes; the empty sickness in his stomach which made him stretch his arms between his knees; the sudden nausea when a boy from another class came into the room. As he washed for lunch, his hands and face seemed dry as if they rejected the water. The fact of his lie remained like a weight in him.

At any moment a boy might say to him 'Westy wants to see you', and the thought made him cold amid their laughter and talking. He moved remotely among them and the time seemed past for ever when he ran with them down the path by the artichokes or took the gate which Scott held open after rugger. The Dormouse had swayed him before the window of the fifth form room and he remembered with a shock, which for an instant was keener than his dread, that he had never gone to look at his drawings. The lie had made that impossible and he wondered whether the Dormouse had missed him and had wished that he had gone. As he thought of the past he was sorry that he had not been more friendly to the Dormouse, as if he stood already at the moment which would end it.

Mr Western was not in his place at lunch and Dago said grace. Randal felt secretly responsible for the absence as if nothing could again be normal until he was punished. The noise in the hall seemed strange without Westy, and the empty chair at the prefects' table frightened and sickened him with guilt. His anxiety increased. He felt trapped by the slow accuracy of the meal while outside Westy acted against him. He could not stir. He needed only two minutes away from them. His mind became fixed on that short time which could save him from the course of events which now filled him with terror. Two minutes might still elapse before the interview. He swallowed the last of his food. He dared not think of what might happen if he had no time to persuade them that he was ill. Perhaps his parents would be summoned. He would be expelled. The others elbowed him back as they pushed rowdily to the door.

He went straight to the Linen Room. Matron was there. She began speaking to him.

'You're the boy I want, Thane. I've spoken to Mr Western and he'll see you in the morning. He's had to be away from school to-day. That's all. He says you're to go on with your lessons as usual until he sees you.'

'Matron I—'

'Well, what is it? There's no more to be said. I can't help you.'

'I think I'm ill, Matron. I get headaches and I can't sleep at night. I haven't slept at all for about a week. I think I've got insomnia.'

He felt no more responsible for himself. He believed that all that he might now do was uncontrollable, and his next words expressed his lawless world.

'Can I have a sleeping draught, Matron? Can I have some bromide?'

He asked for what he believed to be an unmentionable drug. In this way he declared his retreat from their world of realities. He was absorbed in his atmosphere of illness while Matron was speaking.

'—So you had better sleep again in the Sick Room to-night. I shall come in before I go to bed and make sure you're all right. If you're really ill—'

He heard only 'sleep again in the Sick Room'. He knew with startling clarity that it was the reason that he had come. He wanted more than anything else to sleep in the Sick Room. His danger would be brought there to peace and nothing could hurt him. As he left the Linen Room he seemed to possess a secret whence he had gained from them, without their knowledge, the rest of that day and night.

He spent the evening, after the lessons of the afternoon when the sun had sunk slowly at the tall windows of the classrooms, in wandering about the corridors and stairs. Some of the lights were on and the air was very warm. He seemed to move in the earlier time of his childhood, aware of the good and the innocence concealed in him and he felt, strangely in those bleak places where he had once known only grief, empowered and surrounded with love. He seemed to be no longer in the school and to move unconsciously as in a dream. His face was flushed and calm and he breathed deeply. He waited for the night. He felt within him a feverish anticipation like a boy who hangs the Chinese lanterns before a longed-for party. An unformed idea haunted and bewildered him which convinced him that the next day did not exist and that he could not again awake to the lie. He scarcely saw the walls of the corridors and he did not feel the worn banisters of the stairs. He seemed already transported to the night ahead in the Sick Room which curiously protected him. The bell rang through the building. He went at last across the landing and down the lit dormitory corridor with its white doors and up the stairs to the Sick Room. He felt a proud excitement, as if all would there be answered as at an assignation with a lover. He switched on the light in the empty room.

The room had long been dark except for the open square of window and the tiny skylight in the bevelled cheek of a water jug. Randal lay in the bed near the fireplace and listened. He heard no sound of a footstep nor a clock nor a door opening and even the window was quiet. He strained to listen, then relaxed and listened again. The absence of sound closed on him and fell away like the swell of a lake. He played with the hypnotizing sensation, which was what he had wanted, until he realized that he could do that all night. The silence would remain and nothing could interrupt him. He could sleep or be awake, move or lie still and the hours would pass, like a bare gap, to the morning and the lie. He sat up. His eyes were round and open to the night as if he challenged some living form to touch him. The room with its three other beds and the four wash-bowls appeared malignly empty. The window which should have been black was already grey. There was little time. His mind cleared and he knew that he must move.

He drew back the bedclothes and swung his leg over the side of his bed. His face watched the window and he listened. From beneath where the school was sleeping no sound came. He stood on the lino-leum and he went with curiosity to the window. As he passed between the washstand and the three unmade beds he seemed to inspect the room like someone taking stock of his domain before a decisive action. He stretched his arms to the stone mullions and raised himself between them. He stood on the ledge. His hands grasped the rough mullions clumsily and his toes curled from the cold stone. The window seemed solid and real above the airy fall to the terrace. He thought how he could lose his balance and fall like a weight into that light space. He looked down and wondered. The hush of the night was everywhere around. The gravel of the road showed grey beside the white railings, and the huge chestnut over the gate to the Paddock was warm with darkness. A breeze from the plain touched his face and stirred his hair and the sleeves and trousers of his pyjamas, and he shivered. He felt giddy and he longed for the warmth of the great branches. He turned his face quickly and he knew that he could not yet go back to his bed.

He climbed from the window and stood again in the room. Then he went to the door, opened it and closed it softly behind him. He groped his way down the passage. His eyes were full of darkness and he moved purposefully like a sleep-walker. He went down the narrow stairs. From the end of the dormitory corridor the gas jet flickered along the beeswaxed floor. He walked toward it. He saw his striped flannel pyjamas and his bare feet in the stream of light, and he was frightened to be alone and awake in the silent building where everyone was asleep.

He stood at the last door by the Linen Room. The gas jet cast its warm light on his black hair and his pale intent face with the closed lips. He gripped the door handle and turned it. A wave of fright rose and sank in his body. He shuddered and loosened his lips and frowned in anger. He pushed open the door and went into the dormitory.

A faint light fell from the opened windows on the two rows of beds. He went to the prefect's bed at the far end of the room where Felton slept. He stood beside him. Felton was turned away and his fair hair was brushed from the cold light of a window. His throat was bare. His lips were parted in his sleep and his smooth and even face was fresh with the cool breeze, which did not stir the lashes of his closed eyelids. Shadow lay under his eyes and at the corners of his mouth and in the dent of the pillow beneath his head. A hand held the sheet against his bared chest through the unbuttoned jacket of his pyjamas, and the creases of his loosely curved fingers showed minutely with the marks of dirt in his small square finger-nails. He had only the sheet over him because of the warmth and his straight and relaxed body showed in the half light as if he were naked. Randal gazed at Felton, where he had never before seen him, with an intensity and for so long that he seemed to dream of him. His eyes hurt with the desire to end Felton and at the same time wholly to possess him, until at last they drew him to where he lay. He sank on the bed with his arms on either side of Felton. He laid his hand across the mouth for silence, and the lips were full and soft against his palm. He slid his hands over the flutter of the eyelids to cover the eyes. The nose and mouth were clear under his mask of hands. Felton gripped his wrists and drew back his fingers into the thick hair. He thus pulled Randal on to him, and he lay over Felton's firm body and felt his warmth beat upwards to him. His hands were clenched in the ruffled hair and he gazed absorbed into Felton's eyes. The blood knocked through his body and blinded him. He pressed his lips on Felton's mouth. Felton stirred, and Randal remained motionless. His search and his desire were for the instant forgotten for they had momentarily become that action.

Someone was standing in the open door. Randal did not move. He heard Matron say:

'Go back to the Sick Room, Thane. Wait there in the morning.'

He got up from the bed. He went between the two rows of beds towards Matron. His mind was clear as when he had awoken from the dream of killing Felton. He knew neither misery nor joy but confidence. As he went past Matron and out of the dormitory he seemed to possess in his every vein something irrevocable and of more value than anything that he had known.

PART SIX

Common Entrance

Randal went to Mr Western's study after breakfast which had been brought to him in the Sick Room. The fire was splintering in the tidy grate and a white morning mist shone in the window. The study was like the breakfast-room of a big white hotel at Plymouth when the haze lay bright on the sea, the first morning in Navy Week. Randal, conscious of himself and his clothes, walked to the window and looked out over the terrace. Through the mist he could see the grey mass of the chestnut, the tall flagpole and the railings. He coughed into his unclenched hand which was fringed by the sweater like a man's cuff. He turned and rested his fingers on the mantelshelf. His shoes were cleaned, his stockings neat and he missed only the long trousers and the shirt and tie. He glanced at the barometer near the fireplace. The reflection showed the composure of his forehead from which his hair was brushed aside. He stared at himself, knowing with satisfaction the calm in his handsome features, the quiet in his throat which would give his voice control, the grace of his movements. He was grown up and honest and patient. He watched Mr Western seriously when he came in and closed the door.

Randal sat leaning towards the fire with his hands clasped between his knees. Westy sat at his desk to his right. Randal could feel his intent gaze on his shoulder so that he dared not move and only turned his head from the fire to the window. Westy was disappointing. He did not talk in the way that Randal had planned but was obscure and dull and mentioned actions which no longer interested him. He almost spoiled his own serious attitude. It was not important. His tranquil gaze fell from the window towards the fire. He wanted to leave the school and begin anew.

'—It appears you went to Matron and said you were ill. To explain why you didn't want to bathe perhaps? – At half-past ten she went to the Sick Room. It was when she found you were not there and was returning past the dormitories that she saw the door open – I don't wish to frighten you but—'

Randal scarcely listened. He had tried to follow but soon began to say 'I don't believe a word of it,' and as the voice continued he repeated to himself 'Pompous old ass – Pompous old ass – Pompous old ass' for the sake of a change. The incongruity of his gay mocking refrain amongst Westy's solemn words amused him. It would pass the time until he could go.

'—I told Felton that he must on no account speak to you—'

Pompous old ass – Pompous old ass – Pompous –

'—Nothing can be gained either for us or for you by your remaining after this term. Obviously a scholarship is out of the question. I've written to your father and told him that I considered it better for you to take the Common Entrance this term and go to Landscott in September – That is all I have to say. I'm sorry that—'

Randal left the study. He felt bored and there was no one whom he wanted to see. He strolled along the corridor and into the Lobby where he began to read, carefully and with complete detachment, the school list. Adams, Anderson, Andrewes, Bates – What did it matter? Nothing could disturb him now. He put his hands in his pockets and went along the passage, waiting for the bell.

During the weeks that passed before the Common Entrance examination Randal took a different interest in his work. His ignorance, from which he believed that he had suffered, was gone. He especially liked Latin with its strange architectural order, the intricacies of which he quickly mastered. He arranged his books in his locker as on a library shelf. He was filled with a sense of purpose. If he spoke to anyone it was usually to ask whether he had seen the Dormouse, for only with him could he know the pleasure of equality and could watch the concentration of his eyes and hand, as he continued to draw during the lengthening evenings which they spent together. The Dormouse came to rely on his friendship. On their free afternoons they went for long walks and sometimes as far as

Trelawney Hill. These walks far from the school gave Randal the same delight as his Latin compositions. When they were finished he soon forgot them and awaited the next, and he felt an achievement as if he had moved forward. Time, with the Spring in the hills and on the plain, was passing.

They stood on Trelawney Hill, looking towards the sea. The sky was plain blue and cloudless and, miles beyond the distinguishable countryside, a thin line drew the limit of a rougher blue. Randal breathed the air direct from the sea and sands. His eyes tightened as if he narrowed them against the sea-light, searching for the glimpse of a sail or full rigged ship on a distant horizon. He sang aloud words of crazy release.

> 'Far and few, far and few
>> Are the lands where the Jumblies live;
> Their heads are green, and their hands are blue,
>> And they went to sea in a sieve.'

He laughed and looked at the Dormouse. He felt liberated, as he had when a small child escaping miraculously across the seven seas, the unique possessor of the silver and the golden talisman. He was very happy and turning again he called the gay verses, with no regret, over the land at their feet.

> 'I had a little nut-tree,
>> Nothing would it bear
> But a silver nutmeg
>> And a golden pear.

> The King of Spain's daughter
>> Came to visit me,
> All for the sake
>> Of my little nut-tree.

> I skipped over ocean
>> I danced over sea

And all the birds in the air
  Couldn't catch me.'

The sun streamed to him over the fields and the farms and the roads.

'God,' he said, 'I shall be glad to leave.'

'Why?' the Dormouse said.

'I shall be free.'

The Dormouse stared at him where they stood on the edge of the land. Randal's face was tinged with the sun to his rich curling black hair. He seemed older and stronger than him and his legs were firm on the earth as if he owned it. Yet the Dormouse sensed about his eyes and the sharp curve of his mouth an anxiety which belied his elation. He was sad at his words and at the same time alarmed, as if Randal had already gone and the light had sunk from the world where they had lived together and he must soon leave too. He felt immeasurably alone. For an instant the prospect of the future and their separate lives fell like a shadow across his mind.

'Will you ever come back?' he said.

'No,' Randal said. 'I don't want to come back.'

They turned and went from the hill. The sun sank above their heads in the valleys, where the air was warm and green with the scent of ferns and the boughs of trees. The Dormouse walked slowly. He thought, as might a man of experience, of the time when he would never see or know Randal again. He hardly looked at the plants and leaves as they passed. Randal walked ahead. He seemed to hold something which no one else possessed, and what that was he did not ask. He looked carefully at everything as if to memorize it for the last time before a journey.

The three days of the Common Entrance examination, which took place in the first floor Library at the masters' end of the building, had a privileged and timeless atmosphere. Randal enjoyed being a 'candidate' which separated him from the others. He took his place, each morning and afternoon, at the big table on which the ink pots, the pens and the blotting-paper were neatly set. He shifted the blotting-paper, tested the pen and moved the ink pot closer as if he attended a conference. Each day the old invigilator sat so comfortably in his shabby clothes that it was impossible to think of his taking them off, while behind him the summer lay hot on the worn stone of the window-ledge. When he had finished a paper Randal crossed it from his list, counted the number that remained and packed up his answers. He opened his book squarely before him and stared through the window into the heat which seemed to tick slowly by as if there were no place for night. He would fix on a shine of glass, miles distant, pretending easily that it was Spain, with Greece and the Hellespont in the infinite blue lines beyond, and he was Jason plunging through the torrent in sandals fresh and wet or with the Golden Fleece in the hot white streets of Thessaly. Or away on the plain to his left he would see a gold church vane amongst a great crowing of cockerels and barking and shouting, and then he was a Mountebank calling his wares through the streets of Troy or the markets of Baghdad, avoiding the gaudily robed Merchants and Princes, or perhaps a Prince himself. Always there was sunlight and the distances of the world to be travelled, in endless freedom, like that Yellow-Dog Dingo. In those hours where time lay fallow and he waited for his papers to be collected, his life lay like a dream around him.

When the Common Entrance was over, Randal had no more to do. He sat behind the form and read or, when Little Willie had an hour free, he took Randal with him into the garden. They chose a corner in the full heat of the sun and where the plain stretched below them. Little Willie opened one of the books which he had brought, Pre-Raphaelite poems or the ballads or more often Tennyson, and asked Randal to read aloud. Randal, with his back and head against the grass bank, was then aware only of the modulations of his voice and the feeling of the syllables passing from his tongue to his lips.

> '—And drunk delight of battle with my peers,
> Far on the ringing plains of windy Troy.
> I am a part of all that I have met—'

The sense of the words only vaguely touched him, entranced by the sound and power of Ulysses.

'—for my purpose holds
To sail beyond the sunset, and the baths
Of all the western stars, until I die.
It may be that the gulfs will wash us down:
It may be we shall touch the Happy Isles,
And see the great Achilles, whom we knew—'

The light dazzled him where his hand shaded his eyes and the book, which he read almost drowsily. The hum of the insects in the garden round him mingled with the farther noises of the village and the sounds distant over the plain. He had forgotten where he was. Little Willie heard the same sounds beyond Randal's treble voice, while he watched his elbow, propping from his knees his bowed head, and the movement of his lips with the first dark down. Randal especially liked to read Rossetti's *Sister Helen*, hearing his voice rise and sink to the thrilling verses and their ominous refrain, which fell from his lips as if by its own momentum, like water over pebbles. He scarcely breathed the words and his face was solemn and intent.

'Oh, it's Keith of Eastholm rides so fast,
Sister Helen,
For I know the white mane on the blast.'
'The hour has come, has come at last,
Little brother!'
(*O Mother, Mary Mother,
Her hour at last, between Hell and Heaven!*)'

The book lay hot against his knees, where his fingers marked the white page, on which the light endlessly flickered. Sometimes Little Willie asked him to read the ballad of Lord Rendal whose lover had given him eels, 'spickit and sparkit', to eat and had poisoned him. Little Willie had a sense of finality to hear Randal read this poem with his own name, as if it were about himself. The monotonous chant of the boy's voice, which was yet too young for emphasis, crossed the pure and heat-filled air, in which the story seemed again to be enacted. It merged strangely with his knowledge that Randal soon must leave, and would read to him no more. The voice passed, lightly and with odd simplicity to the last stanza.

> 'What will you give your lover, Rendal, my son?
> What will you give your lover, my pretty one?'
>   'A rope to hang her, Mother!
>   A rope to hang her, Mother!
> Make my bed soon, for I'm sick to my heart,
> And I fain would lie down.'

These hours were a time which Randal would not often remember, although its effect was to last his life, and which Little Willie could not easily forget. The lunch bell rang over the terrace. Randal closed the books and carried them under his arm. They walked together up the steep path between the fruit trees. Randal glanced at the books which he held. Little Willie thought how the summer made him tired. The shadows of the twigs flecked Randal's face and his bared neck and his hand which clasped the books, while Little Willie gazed at him through the dust which they made. His mind was filled with Randal whom he did not want to leave, while he climbed slowly beside him through the garden until they reached the gate to the terrace. So the days passed, and Randal longed more than ever for the train bound for Landscott, away from the school and even The Grange.

One day Westy stopped him by his classroom.

'Thane,' he said, 'I've news for you.'

He gave him a sheet of paper. It was the Common Entrance results from Landscott.

'You've done better than I expected. I'm very pleased.'

Randal read the names. His was fifth on a list of thirty.

'You've done well.'

Randal went down the corridor. That sense of purpose, which he had felt since he left the study, was in part fulfilled.

PART SEVEN

Departure

Randal waited at the junction. A row of trees, which were visited by starlings, passed behind the signal box and continued in the low-lying fields beside the lines. Their leaves had thinned and turned yellow, and through them the bare sky showed grey. The September smell like rust of the leaves and of the damp air, which held back the rain, mixed with that of the smoke and oil in the station. There were few people waiting for the train. Randal walked along the platform, and his calm face watched the screen of young trees as if he were thinking. He was scared. The sensation of cold in his throat increased his sense of elation and detachment, which he enjoyed, and he did not look at the others but kept his eyes on the moist land beyond. He had bought a magazine and had considered buying a novel. He had inquired the time of the train. He was on the right platform. He held his trilby hat by the brim and flicked it against his legs in the long trousers of his grey suit, so that he saw the glint of cuff-links in his striped shirt. His tie was tightly knotted over a brass pin. He had a pound note and he jingled the change in his pocket. At the end of the platform he turned and saw the many wires fence back the shunting sheds and a tall brick chimney-stack. The chill air was new and expectant. He returned to his suitcase and overcoat, and stood above the hard polished lines which narrowed in the level distance. The signal was down. He looked again at the clock. He was fourteen; in three minutes he would be in the train for Landscott.

He lifted his suitcase and moved it forward. On his left a trolley was piled with luggage. In front of it he saw two suitcases on which was a square box strapped in a rug, and against them leaned a hockey stick. He realized that the cases and the hockey stick must belong to a schoolboy. It was naturally someone returning to Landscott. He wondered what kind of a boy he was and hoped that he was pleasant and that they would travel together. He looked down the platform, and there was no other boy among the waiting passengers. He turned again to the trolley which blocked his view. He knew that the boy must be on the other side. He looked at the clock. He had one minute in which to see him. He shifted his suitcase until it overlapped the edge of the platform. There was no sign of the boy, and he moved anxiously as if to find a way through the trolley. His need for him increased and he postponed the thought of his departure behind that more urgent desire. He did not mind if his suitcase were stolen, so that he might see him, nor if he missed the train.

He watched the hockey stick. The tape was grimed with sweat where hands had grasped it during the game. He wanted to hold or borrow it. He wanted, if he could have known, a friend who would give him, until his death, no rest. He saw an arm, in a tight blue serge sleeve, reach from behind the trolley. The hand took the strap binding the box. The fingers were thrust taut into the rug by the thumb and palm which gripped the strap. They were small and neat and strong. The hand, with its every minute clear line, was familiar. Warmth flooded from his stomach through his throat and to his head as if he drowned. He could not tell where he was. He felt the hands grip his wrists and drag his fingers tightly through thick hair, and the body stir beneath him, and his lips pressed on Felton's mouth. He stared at the hand as if hypnotized. Some powerful impulse beat in his head. It seemed that Felton stood within reach, on his side of the trolley, and that he could touch him. He scarcely knew whether it was fact or a dream. The roar of the train approached. His loss of Felton hit him and weakened him so that he was appalled that he had not known it before. The train crashed past him and drew up and the doors were flung open. A young girl, in a blue serge uniform, came from behind the trolley. She held the strapped box. Her right hand swung the hockey stick. Randal did not look at her face. A sense of deprivation and at the same time of relief swept through his body and took his breath. He picked up his suitcase and overcoat, and got into an empty compartment.

The train moved out of the junction. Randal sat in a corner, with his chin rested on his hand, and gazed through the window. He felt alert as if for a long time he had not eaten. His mind was free of responsibility, and he had no desires; his face was composed as he watched the passing country. He forgot himself and seemed to be neither there nor anywhere but rather a part of what he saw. The thin line of trees rippled with their yellow or tarnished leaves over the glass-like marsh, while beyond them the low green hills rose and fell, and kept an even distance from the track. He was filled with an extraordinary knowledge of himself and of the permanence of his life. Felton, who stood radiant above the combe of snow or held him in his arms amid the glimmering waste beside the black edge of the wood, lived in the same moment as that frieze of heroes at whom he gazed by the dying light of the nursery fire. The love which he had felt for them was the same, and could not alter. The trees seemed to wind with them through his eyes. He knew that he need no longer search for Felton, for he already possessed him. He knew no more anxiety. His eyes were fixed exultantly on the trees moving over the glittering marsh, as if he watched a crystal, within which his own life and the movements and the being of Felton gradually became ordered. He heard only the symmetry of words which they had become and which he held within him. His face and smiling lips were lit by the autumn land, as he waited for the poem to form. He took from his pocket his diary and pencil. He began to write. Round him the deserted compartment seemed the only place that he had ever inhabited while the regular beat of the train, which carried him forward, was like a distant and unheeded echo. His words moved in triumph across the page while he thought of Felton against the flickering leaves. The poem and Felton possessed his mind. The two patterns of his life were achieved.

Penguin Modern Classics

OFFICERS AND GENTLEMEN
EVELYN WAUGH

'A literary innovator, inventor of modern black comedy in the novel'
Malcolm Bradbury, *Mail on Sunday*

Guy Crouchback is now attached to a Commando unit undergoing training on
the Hebridean Isle of Mugg, where the whisky flows freely and HM forces have
to show proper respect for the omnipotent Laird. But the high comedy of Mugg
is followed by the bitterness of Crete – and the chaos and indignity of total
withdrawal or surrender.

Officers and Gentlemen is the second volume of Waugh's trilogy, *Sword of Honour*,
which chronicles the fortunes of Guy Crouchback. The first and third volumes, *Men
at Arms* and *Unconditional Surrender*, are also published in Penguin.

Penguin Modern Classics

UNCONDITIONAL SURRENDER
EVELYN WAUGH

'Arguably the best British prose fiction to come out of the Second World War' Will Self, *Independent*, on *Sword of Honour*

Guy Crouchback lost his Halberdier idealism. A desk job in London gives him the chance of reconciliation with his former wife. Then, in Yugoslavia, as a liaison officer with the Partisans, he finally becomes aware of the futility of a war he once saw in terms of honour.

Unconditional Surrender is the final volume of Waugh's *Sword of Honour* trilogy, which chronicles the fortunes of Guy Crouchback. The first and second volumes, *Men at Arms* and *Officers and Gentlemen*, are also published in Penguin.

PENGUIN MODERN CLASSICS

WILD ANALYSIS
SIGMUND FREUD

Translated by Alan Bance

With an Introduction by Adam Phillips

'These papers represent his most significant contributions to the subject over three decades' Adam Phillips

This powerful volume brings together Freud's major writings on psychoanalytic method and the question of psychoanalytic technique.

The fundamental concern of these works is the complex relationship between patient and analyst. Here Freud explores both the crucial importance of and the huge risks involved in patients' transference of their emotions on to their therapist. He also shows the ambiguous dangers of 'wild analysis' by doctors who are insufficiently trained or offer instant solutions; looks at issues such as the length of a treatment; and offers a trenchant discussion of the controversy surrounding psychoanalysis as a medical discipline. And, in examining the tensions between the practice of psychoanalysis and its central theory – the disruptive nature of the unconscious – Freud asks, can there ever really be rules for analysis?

General Editor: Adam Phillips

Penguin Modern Classics

THE UNCANNY
SIGMUND FREUD

Screen Memories / Leonardo da Vinci and a Memory of his Childhood / Family Romances / Creative Writers and Daydreaming / The Uncanny

Translated by David McLintock

With an Introduction by Hugh Haughton

'Freud ... ultimately did more for our understanding of art than any other writer since Aristotle' Lionel Trilling

Freud was fascinated by the mysteries of creativity and the imagination. The major pieces collected here explore the vivid but seemingly trivial childhood memories that often 'screen' far more uncomfortable desires; the links between literature and daydreaming – and our intensely mixed feelings about things we experience as 'uncanny'.

His insights into the roots of artistic expression in the triangular 'family romances' (of father, mother and infant) that so dominate our early lives, and the parallels between our own memories and desires and the tormented career of a genius like Leonardo, reveal the artistry of Freud's own writing.

General Editor: Adam Phillips

PENGUIN MODERN CLASSICS

THE JOKE AND ITS RELATION TO THE UNCONSCIOUS
SIGMUND FREUD

Translated by Joyce Crick

With an Introduction by John Carey

'Daring ... brilliant and convincing' John Carey

Why do we laugh? The answer, argued Freud in this groundbreaking study of humour, is that jokes, like dreams, satisfy our unconscious desires.

The Joke and Its Relation to the Unconscious (1905) explains how jokes provide immense pleasure by releasing us from our inhibitions and allowing us to express sexual, aggressive, playful or cynical instincts that would otherwise remain hidden. In elaborating this theory, Freud brings together a rich collection of puns, witticisms, one-liners and anecdotes, many of which throw a vivid light on the society of early twentieth-century Vienna. Jokes, as Freud shows, are a method of giving ourselves away.

General Editor: Adam Phillips

PENGUIN MODERN CLASSICS

HENDERSON THE RAIN KING
SAUL BELLOW

'A kind of wildly delirious dream made real by the force of Bellow's rollicking prose and the offbeat inventiveness of his language' Chicago Tribune

Bellow evokes all the rich colour and exotic customs of a highly imaginary Africa in this comic novel about a middle-aged American millionaire who, seeking a new, more rewarding life, descends upon an African tribe. Henderson's awesome feats of strength and his unbridled passion for life win him the admiration of the tribe – but it is his gift for making rain that turns him from mere hero into messiah.

A hilarious, often ribald story, *Henderson the Rain King* is also a profound look at the forces that drive a man through life.

WINNER OF THE NOBEL PRIZE FOR LITERATURE

PENGUIN MODERN CLASSICS

HERZOG
SAUL BELLOW

With an Introduction by Malcolm Bradbury

'Spectacular ... surely Bellow's greatest novel' Malcolm Bradbury

This is the story of Moses Herzog, a great sufferer, joker, mourner and charmer. Although his life steadily disintegrates around him – he has failed as a writer and teacher, as a father, and has lost the affection of his wife to his best friend – Herzog sees himself as a survivor, both of his private disasters and those of the age. He writes unsent letters to friends and enemies, colleagues and famous people, revealing his wry perception of the world and the innermost secrets of his heart.

'A masterpiece ... Herzog's voice, for all its wildness and strangeness and foolishness, is the voice of a civilization, our civilization'
The New York Times Book Review

WINNER OF THE NOBEL PRIZE FOR LITERATURE

PENGUIN MODERN CLASSICS

JUNKY
WILLIAM S. BURROUGHS

'Reads today as fresh and unvarnished as it ever has' Will Self

Burroughs' first novel – a largely autobiographical account of the constant cycle of drug dependency, cures and relapses – remains the most unflinching, unsentimental account of addiction ever written. Through junk neighbourhoods in New York, New Orleans and Mexico City, through time spent kicking, time spent dealing and time rolling drunks for money, through junk sickness and a sanatorium, *Junky* is a field report (by a writer trained in anthropology at Harvard) from the American post-war drug underground. A cult classic, it has influenced generations of writers with its raw, sparse and unapologetic tone. This definitive edition painstakingly recreates the author's original text word for word.

PENGUIN MODERN CLASSICS

THE WILD BOYS
WILLIAM S. BURROUGHS

'Burroughs's boldest experiment and, perhaps, finest achievement'
Los Angeles Times

In this funny, nightmarish masterpiece of imaginative excess, grotesque characters engage in acts of violent one-upmanship, boundless riches mangle a corner of Africa into a Bacchanalian utopia, and technology, flesh and violence fuse with and undo each other. A fragmentary, freewheeling novel, it sees wild boys engage in vigorous, ritualistic sex and drug taking, as well as pranksterish guerrilla warfare and open combat with a confused and outmatched army. *The Wild Boys* shows why Burroughs is a writer unlike any other, able to make captivating the explicit and horrific.

'An ethereally beautiful book' *Rolling Stone*

PENGUIN MODERN CLASSICS

EXTERMINATOR!
WILLIAM S. BURROUGHS

'The only American novelist writing today who may conceivably be possessed of genius' Norman Mailer

A man, dispirited by ageing, endeavours to steal a younger man's face; a doctor yearns for a virus that might eliminate his discomfort by turning everyone else into doubles of himself; a Colonel lays out the precepts of the life of DE (Do Easy); conspirators posthumously succeed in blowing up a train full of nerve gas; a mandrill known as the Purple Better One runs for the presidency with brutal results; and the world drifts towards apocalypses of violence, climate and plague. The hallucinatory landscape of William Burroughs' compellingly bizarre, fragmented novel is constantly shifting, something sinister always just beneath the surface.

PENGUIN MODERN CLASSICS

THE SOUND OF TRUMPETS
JOHN MORTIMER

When a Tory MP is found dead in a swimming pool wearing a leopardskin bikini, the embittered Leslie (now Lord) Titmuss sees the ideal opportunity to re-enter the political arena. All he needs is a puppet, and Terry Flitton – inoffensive New Labourite – is perfect. Along with his beautiful, very PC wife, Terry heads blindly for the Hartscombe and Worsfield South by-election. But is he too busy listening for the sound of victory trumpets to notice that the Tory dinosaur is not quite extinct?

John Mortimer's brilliant follow-up to *Paradise Postponed* and *Titmuss Regained*, *The Sound of Trumpets* is a devilishly witty satire on political ambition, spin and sleaze, and the culmination of a masterly trilogy.

'Delicious ... Mortimer in vintage form' *Observer*

'A thumping good plot ... Titmuss is one of the writer's finest creations' *Sunday Telegraph*

Contemporary ... Provocative ... Outrageous ... Prophetic ... Groundbreaking ... Funny ... Disturbing ... Different ... Moving ... Revolutionary ... Inspiring ... Subversive ... Life-changing ...

What makes a modern classic?

At Penguin Classics our mission has always been to make the best books ever written available to everyone. And that also means constantly redefining and refreshing exactly what makes a 'classic'. That's where Modern Classics come in. Since 1961 they have been an organic, ever-growing and ever-evolving list of books from the last hundred (or so) years that we believe will continue to be read over and over again.

They could be books that have inspired political dissent, such as *Animal Farm*. Some, like *Lolita* or *A Clockwork Orange*, may have caused shock and outrage. Many have led to great films, from *In Cold Blood* to *One Flew Over the Cuckoo's Nest*. They have broken down barriers – whether social, sexual, or, in the case of *Ulysses*, the boundaries of language itself. And they might – like *Goldfinger* or *Scoop* – just be pure classic escapism. Whatever the reason, Penguin Modern Classics continue to inspire, entertain and enlighten millions of readers everywhere.

'No publisher has had more influence on reading habits than Penguin'
Independent

'Penguins provided a crash course in world literature'
Guardian

The best books ever written